Cat Ranch

Judith Read

Cat Ranch

Copyright © 2020 by Judith Read

eISBN 978-1-9990405-2-9
ISBN 978-1-9990405-1-2

Cover Design: Scott Holmes & Infinite Pathways Press

1 2 3 4 5 6 7 8 9 10

BOOKS BY JUDITH READ

The Boomer Years: Reflections

Cat Ranch

DEDICATION

This work of fiction is dedicated to the real-life volunteers in cat rescue agencies everywhere. They support and advocate for those creatures who cannot speak for themselves.

God bless you all.

ACKNOWLEDGEMENTS

This book was inspired by the kindness and love of two people who shared their home and hearts to nine rescued cats. They happen to be my daughter and son-in-law, Jennifer Read and Brent Tarabalka.

The creation of this story has been a long, sometimes frustrating journey. Without the support, guidance and encouragement of the following people, you would not be reading it now.

Thanks to my cousin, Karen Thompson, an avid reader, who went over the early drafts and laughed in all the right places. Erika Lee, a dear friend and English whiz who made necessary early corrections, my youngest daughter, Brynne Read, and her friend, Amanda Boetto, who provided a much needed millennial's point of view, Barry Gottlieb of The Hamilton Writers' Guild, who graciously shared his writing expertise with me, Shane Clair, a fine writer himself, who told me not to be so hard on myself, Janice J. Richardson, an established author, and my cheerleader, MJ Moores, a new friend, author, editor and indie author coach who was able to show me how to pull it all together in a very professional way; and special thanks to my dear friend, artist/animator, Scott Holmes who created the amazing book cover.

I would also like to mention my feline friends, the Crew; Montana, Haylow, Joey, Spruce, Nukkers, Snappy, Hermie, Sarge, and of course Winklin, who'll always be Winky to me.

THE CREW

SNAPPY

JOEY

NUKKERS

HAYLOW

WINKLIN

MONTANA

SPRUCE

SARGE

HERMIE

"What's New Pussy Cat?"

~Burt Bacharach and Hal David, 1965

CHAPTER ONE

"These jeans definitely make me look fat!" I scowled at my reflection in Donna's floor-length hall mirror. My good friend's chuckle echoed from the kitchen, while I recalled my nightclub dance debacle of the previous evening.

"Oh, Reggie, you're getting paranoid! You were wearing black silk pants with a hip-length tunic. The dance floor was filled with distracted geriatrics!" she called out to me, then strolled down her hall to stand beside me.

"I'm sure no one in that crowd could see well enough to notice that you ripped the butt of your pants!" She slipped a slim arm around my sagging shoulders and continued her attempt to humour me.

"Not even Frankie Valli noticed, or I'm sure he would have made a public announcement," she joked. "Look at it this way. You were the dancing queen! Considering your bad knee, and the fact that you were still able to get out of the guest bed today, I'd say that's pretty damned good. Jeez, we haven't danced that much since Abba took the boat over from Sweden."

"It was a plane," I corrected, twisting around to check my rear. I frowned at it. She swept back her shoulder-length hair and scrutinized me.

"Whatever. I'm glad they came. I read somewhere that they were the first group to come from a non-English speaking country to have consistent success in the charts of English-speaking countries. Incredible."

She crossed her arms over her chest and leaned back against the wall to watch me. At this point, I didn't care if Abba sang in Latin. I made my solemn pledge.

"I am going on a strict diet starting today. Maybe Keto." I sucked in my gut, pulling my yellow jersey over my thighs. She regarded me with a wry smile.

"Don't be silly. You've always had a sturdy, athletic build. You look great, period. I too took full advantage of that smorgasbord. Why not? It was awesome. There were so many exotic dishes and everything was so healthy. And how about the club decor? Just like a scene from Hollywood. All those flashing strobe lights, all those rich, glitzy people dolled up for the town, all those pearls and diamonds…"

"All those Botoxed faces." I interrupted with a sly grin. She stifled a laugh with her hand, then lost her balance. I caught her by one arm, my humour restored.

"It was a fantastic evening, lots of cool memories and great oldies. As usual, I had a blast. Thanks for making it happen, girlfriend."

She turned away from the mirror and cocked her head at me, eyebrows raised. "Comp tickets? With my best friend? No question there. Too bad we didn't score some dough in the casino though. What would you do with $100,000?"

I hesitated, then shot a bold look into the nasty mirror.

"Go to a fancy fat farm." I opened my arms wide in an Al Jolson parody, not daring to go down on one knee as he did. Donna doubled over, her shoulders shaking. Comically, I was on a roll. We sashayed side by side toward the welcome waft of freshly perked coffee.

Bright shafts of early-morning sun spilled across the creamy parson's table, the scene of many consultations over the years. I collapsed onto my usual high-backed chair and admired the panoramic view from the fifth floor of Donna's Spanish style condo.

3

From her spacious balcony, it was possible to see the immense curve in the Niagara River as it neared its final destination to Lake Ontario. I'd always loved the picturesque village of Niagara-on-the-Lake, but as it turned out, I seemed better suited to Niagara Falls. My two-bedroom condo, in a quiet residential setting, was set well away from the hustle and bustle of the downtown tourist industry. The rents were more affordable too.

Donna busily browsed through a few of the local trade papers when I turned away from the autumn splendour.

"So, Reggie,"—she looked over the advertisements—"How would you like to spend our day together? There's that big craft show out in Vineland. It's their nineteenth year..." Her voice trailed off as she moved briskly toward the bluestone counter. The coffee carafe and two waiting mugs sat neatly arranged on a white wicker tray. After pouring steaming java into my cup, she paused with it midair, waiting for me to take it.

This was a big decision. Or rather, I acted like it was just to get her goat. I pooched out my lips and assumed a frown of deep concentration.

"Hmmm." I closed my eyes as I drew out the m's. My idea didn't include craft shows. I opened my peepers, then said, "After due consideration, I have to tell you that I am thinking more of Jordan Village. Trendy bright boutiques and quaint little art shops to wander through at leisure, followed by a delectable patio lunch along a shady, tree-lined street. I know you like zigzagging your way through throngs of pushy people ogling stalls of overpriced items, but paying to get in?" I made a look of distaste with my mouth, then feigned interest in the wall clock behind her.

"Oh, don't be so cheap!" she scolded. "It's an adventure. You may find a treasure you've wanted all your life."

She turned back to the counter and deftly poured her own brew.

I blew out a sigh over my drink.

"Like a hand-carved back scratcher or a dried collage of a hundred dead leaves?" I groaned.

Donna was a fan of the collage art form. Not me. They looked too disorganized. She stopped and gave me her signature look; hands hip-planted, blond head to one side, blue eyes direct and unblinking.

"You have something against leaves? You just don't appreciate the beauty of nature. It's fall, Reggie. This is the season of all kinds of leaves. Crafters are artisans. They spend many painstaking hours making one-of-a-kind creations…"

"Until somebody else copies their idea." I interrupted. This was fun.

Donna rolled her eyes and went back to savouring her coffee, a gourmet mocha blend that was to die for. I lifted mine gently to my lips, anticipating its delectable flavour. Suddenly she smacked the table. I flinched and spilled.

"Okay, Miss Obstinance," she declared, handing me a napkin. "Why don't I drag you through a beautiful autumn outing in Vineland, where we can inhale the fragrance of mulled apple cider, admire the rich hues of falling leaves, and seek out a one-of-a-kind creation for me. Then, and only then, you can get your composure back over a luscious merlot at lunch in Jordan Village. I'll even pay your admission to the craft show."

Satisfied, she lounged back on her chair, giving me the evil eye.

I was ready to begrudgingly concede to her diplomatic suggestion when a cell phone chimed. My mouth fell open.

"It's mine!" I cried out, digging the red rectangle out of my overburdened bag. "Who would be calling me on a Saturday morning?"

Donna put her coffee down and pointed one

fuchsia nail to the phone screen.

"Isn't there a display number?" she frowned at the phone. I nodded. "There is, but I can't be bothered rooting through my mess of a purse for my reading glasses. What the heck, I'll take it." I peered at the screen. "Probably just a telemarketer anyway. Hello? My eyes darted to Donna's while I waited for the hard sell. There were few beats of silence, then a woman's loud wail.

"Mom! I don't know what to do!"

I sighed. "Lisa," I mouthed to Donna.

This was unusual. Lisa rarely called me. She texted, which wasn't my favourite thing in the world, so this had to be her idea of an urgent situation. Donna, who knew Lisa well, pointed to my phone and whispered "speaker," an impish grin lighting up her face. I nodded at our conspiracy, pressed the speaker button and propped the phone against a vase of pink roses.

"What happ…?" I started to say, but Lisa's panicked voice cut me off.

"It's Grace! She's sick! She can't come here to look after the cats!"

I bit my bottom lip and raised my eyes to the ceiling. Donna's grin was like the Cheshire Cat's, as she settled back for the show. I pictured Lisa's unfortunate cat sitter ailing in bed, with a guilt trip from my daughter adding to her misery. I took my neck in a joking chokehold with my free hand. Donna immediately turned and put her hand over her mouth, stifling her giggles.

"Oh, Lisa. How awful. What's wrong with her?"

"What is wrong is that it couldn't have happened at a worse time!" she huffed. "Brad and I have our cat conference in Toronto today! I already told you, Mom. You don't listen. I'm giving a video presentation on cat safety fencing to one hundred members from all over the GTA. My photo is featured in the Pause for Claws program and Muriel Peabody is counting on me. I can't let her down. I'm a bundle of nerves and now Grace is down with strep throat. I feel sick."

Donna rose from her chair, shaking her head, hand still clamped on her mouth. I was trying to keep a straight face myself.

"Oh, dear! That poor girl. Strep throat is no fun, that's for sure. And now you're left in the lurch."

My little Lisa. I loved her to bits, but she tended toward the dramatic. Her idea of an emergency and mine differed. From her child-like point of view, it could be some dead little critter in her yard that needed to be removed at once, or a man in Canadian

Tire she assumed was stalking her when he mistakenly took her for a sales associate. Fortunately, with years of practice, her easy-going husband, Brad, could diffuse just about any situation, so mother and daughter got along reasonably well.

It was love at first sight for them at the Pause for Claws cat convention eight years ago. Lisa was recovering from a nasty break up with a long-time boyfriend. She grew up with a great love of cats; there always was at least one in our household. Then a splashy ad caught her eye for this Toronto cat show and she decided to get away from her doldrums. In the hospitality room, she literally bumped into Brad and spilt her drink on his suede jacket! As love matches went, they had been blissful ever since.

"Okay, Lisa, take some deep breaths and let me think." I shot a look at Donna who had recovered her composure long enough to plop down on a chair.

I was conflicted. I hadn't seen Donna in two months and we'd been looking forward to having an outing today. I shrugged and mouthed to her, "What do you think?"

A mischievous grin lit up her face and she quickly nodded.

"Well, I did have plans today, Lisa. I don't remember you ever telling me when this conference was. I'm not thrilled in postponing my outing with Donna. I haven't seen her in ages."

Lisa's breathing lightened, then dead silence fell.

"Hello? Lisa? Answer me please." I was getting annoyed. Donna had stopped rocking, her eyes riveted to mine.

"I'm here," she sniffed.

"All right then. It is last minute, but I suppose I can fill in for your sitter. A weak voice broke over the line, "Oh, that would be so great Mom. Brad's out in the garage. I haven't told him yet. I thought I would call you first."

I heaved an exaggerated sigh. Donna wiped the corners of her eyes with a white linen napkin. She gave me a wink and I returned to my distraught child.

"But I'm bringing Donna for company. You guys are in no-man's-land out there. I'll need more than cats for conversation. I guess we'll be staying the night, so give us time to get our stuff together."

"Oh, Mom, thank you!" she squealed, then went on, fully resuscitated. "You have saved me! It would have killed me to let everyone down. Can you come as soon as possible? Like now? It's already nine-thirty and I'll have to go over the cats' diets and activity schedules with you. I don't want to leave anything out or I'll be distracted and unable to concentrate on the presentation tonight," she ended breathlessly.

My mouth hung agape at her nerve. I decided to wrap up the call before I changed my mind.

"We will be there when we arrive, Lisa. Go back to your cat care lists." I snapped the red cover shut.

"Lists?" Donna asked, frowning.

With a deep breath, I returned the phone to my purse.

"You have no idea, but hear me out now that we're heading to a different adventure. Imagine the two of us, ensconced in an exquisite, lodge-like country home, surrounded by tall, lush evergreens with nine, yes, you heard right, nine wonderfully sweet and playful kitties to delight and entertain us."

She hooted while gathering up our empty mugs and spoons from the table.

"Your pitch is irresistible, but what have you gotten us into this time? A fine kettle of fish, or cats rather. And that's what happens to moms right? Only some more than others." She flashed me a quick grin, "And you have been spared the craft show, bitch!"

I laughed.

Donna Cairns, my friend, ready for any possible adventure, if she was available for it. Donna busied herself travelling. We only lived ten miles apart, but it seemed farther as she was frequently away. Our friendship was safe, even if she holidayed in Portugal for two months, our emails and Skype calls kept us in touch. I loved hearing about her latest trek, though travel wasn't really my thing. It didn't take long to get up to date over a two-hour lunch.

It didn't start out that way back in the '60s. We were hung up on the same guy, Todd Ginsberg. A real folkie, with killer blue eyes and a smooth way with the girls. He had a thing for juniors. After we found out he was a two-timer, and we were the two, we centred him out in the main entrance to our high school, teasing him in front of his cool frat buddies. We taunted that he had invited us downstairs to his family rec room to dance to The Archies when no one was home. They'd roared with laughter while he turned red, furiously denying it. Doug Hayslip, another senior, made fun of him calling him a teeny-bopper lover. The guys were having fun cutting up, shoving him around playfully, when Mr. Jantzi, the vice principal appeared, shaking his finger, giving them all a detention. We ran away from the raucous show, hiding in the girl's washroom to giggle. After school, we went to Donna's house and forged our friendship over milk and her mother's famous butter tarts.

I admire Donna so much. She's a giving person

who has volunteered for numerous local charities, her favourite one being the YWCA shelter for homeless women and their children. Donna has an easy grace about her, drawing people to her like a magnet. Being a tall, striking blonde doesn't hurt either.

Her husband Jim passed away two years ago unexpectedly. She was out picking up a few groceries at the local Sobeys for his favourite Thai dinner. Arriving home, she found him collapsed on their living room floor. It turned out to be a massive heart attack, which shocked everyone. Jim was in great shape, a non-smoker, moderate drinker, quick to laugh, larger than life. He was only sixty-two, had just sold his local accounting firm where he had worked for thirty years.

They were planning a long-awaited cruise to Alaska, for their fortieth wedding anniversary. Their only child, Kevin, was in Vancouver teaching at Simon Fraser University when it happened. He was a constant source of comfort and told her after the funeral that he would move back home to be with her. Donna was adamant that he remain on the west coast to be with his partner, Leo. She has kept herself busy, and I think that helped her cope with her loss, but I could see by any sudden distraction, her thoughts far away, that she missed the love of her life.

—o0o—

CHAPTER TWO

I steered my Ford Explorer with care to pull alongside the kitty mailbox on the side of the road to give Donna a closer look. An artist friend of Brad's had painted it as a housewarming gift for the couple. I had been to their remote location three weeks before, just after they moved and offered to help, but Lisa insisted on having everything sorted before she would have me visit again. I smiled at the mailbox and turned into their driveway.

Full, stately evergreens lined the entry up the long leaf-strewn stretch of stone. Further ahead, the bright autumn foliage teemed with lively sparrows, brought to their chirping flight as our tires crunched gravel. We rounded the long curve of the circular drive to behold an impressive, brick Victorian mansion. Even in the bright midday sun, it exuded a look of austerity with a shadowy aura. The upper-level windows had the hooded look of an old crone's eyes.

I could picture a lone, forbidding figure in black

watching our movements below from her vantage point. Mrs. Danvers, of *Rebecca* fame, came to mind. Faded, tattered awnings hung sadly, a testament to a grander era. The imposing rustic porch, supported by gnarled oak posts, was littered with a variety of house-moving detritus. Empty liquor boxes gaped haphazardly around leaning stacks of cardboard totes filling with dead leaves.

The kids had been ecstatic to find such a character home. They had scoured the real estate market for months to locate a good-sized country property that would accommodate their large brood, yet stay within their carefully managed budget.

Lisa told me she knew as soon as she walked through the front door, and saw the spacious centre hall, that she wanted this house more than anything in the world. It was a few miles off the beaten track, but only a short drive to the town of Dunnville.

"Wow!" Donna stared awestruck at the house as her Rockford loafer touched the ground. Her eyes roamed over the ageing English rock garden surrounded by the driveway. Old, wisteria vines wrapped their tendrils around a weathered pergola, its cross timbers scraping the ground. A variety of dried weeds sprouted knee-high, and wind-blown newspapers curled around the bare branches of sparse shrubbery. Layers of leaves covered much of the mossy brick walkway, but it was still possible to see how stunning the gardens could be with considerable effort and expense.

"They'll need a gardener," she laughed ruefully, gesturing around the grounds. I nodded in agreement at the tumbledown scene.

"Hey, ladies!" Brad waved from the front porch. At forty, my son-in-law still reminded me of a husky, well-built teenager, always sporting the latest fashion trends and hairstyles. Although he was Lisa's senior by eight years, at times she seemed older than him. Today, he sported a turquoise and black cotton windbreaker, hair styled in a silver-tipped crewcut.

Lisa's high soprano rang from the kitchen, "Mom, watch the cats when you open the screen. Snappy's just waiting to run out!"

Donna and I navigated our overnight bags and satchels past the doors, careful not to step on the three tabbies weaving around our ankles.

"Hi, Donna!" Lisa squealed. I watched smiling as Donna held out her arms and they hugged tightly.

"Lisa! Good to see you. You look wonderful. And all this"—she looked around the main floor—"is perfect for your kitties."

Brad followed us into a well-appointed country

kitchen to the left of an open staircase. A large island commanded the centre of it. Two big tabbies squirmed playfully on the black granite countertop. Another watchful gray tiger-eyed us from its perch at the top of the stairs. We strolled over to the dining room opposite the kitchen, marvelling at the openness of our surroundings.

They really had managed to do a lot of organizing in three weeks. The art deco dining room suite of oak table, eight chairs, sideboard and china cabinet fit perfectly into the room and complimented the style of the house. A striking Karastan rug in muted shades of taupe and burgundy lent a cozy feel to our surroundings.

Lisa led us to the living room which sprawled from wall to wall at the rear of the house. Thick sunbeams poured through floor-to-ceiling cathedral windows, reflecting off the polished wide-planked floor. Brad's massive study desk, with his trademark banker's rolling chair, occupied one end of the room, while a red Bauhaus sofa, matching chair, and a couple of taupe corduroy retro recliners banked the fieldstone fireplace. Cream French doors opened onto a beautiful cedar deck, running the width of the house. The view from the back of the property was breathtaking. Beyond the yard, the meandering creek boasted a palette of autumn-hewed foliage.

My eyes roamed the living room once more trying to take it all in. Every conceivable cat toy lay strewn about. Pale wicker boxes brimmed over with colourful, crazy, catnip toys. Beige upholstered climbers stood like sentries between the long bank of windows, while fluffy, inviting cat beds displayed on end tables and a glass-topped coffee table. *A spa for cats*, I thought with amusement.

"Donna, this is Winklin."

Startled from my thoughts, I turned to see Lisa lovingly display the resistant orange and white Persian. His single eye glared at me.

Donna gingerly reached out a slender hand to pet the cat. "Oh, poor guy," she cooed. Her fingers withdrew abruptly when his ears flattened and he swiped a paw at her.

Lisa kissed him on the mouth. I winced.

"He can be touchy. Will take his time getting to know you, but he's just a big baby, aren't you boo-boo?" She nuzzled her pretty face into his furry cheek. Winklin was not impressed. He jerked away from her, hissed loudly, then sprang from her arms.

"Just let him come to you, ladies. Trust me. I know it's tempting to hold them close, but the general rule of thumb is to follow a cat's lead. They will let you know what they want. Too often people try to force their own wishes on them. Cats are very independent and intelligent. We need to respect that."

I bit my bottom lip behind Lisa's back, not daring to look at Donna. If only she'd take her own advice.

Lisa turned her attention to the stainless-steel fridge. Its wide door was hidden by typewritten, fluorescent yellow memos, held in perfect placement by cat-paw magnets.

"Their diets and routines are posted here. I know it might seem a little overwhelming, but I wanted to make sure I didn't leave anything out. I would have included our neighbours' phone number in case of an emergency, but they left yesterday for a two-week Caribbean cruise. They are so nice. Janie and Doug. They came to welcome us the day we moved in and have been very helpful. They said if we need anything, feel free to call. People in the country do that you know. They didn't even blink when we told them we had nine indoor cats!"

She bent her small frame to search under a kitchen desk beside Donna.

"I see you hiding, little girl," she chirped.

We peered over her shoulder to find yet another gray tabby, smaller than the others. The cat looked shell shocked.

"What's wrong with that one?" Donna cocked her head to the left. "It looks terrified."

"That's Nukkers," Lisa's voice dropped an octave. "She's timid around the others, especially Winklin. We adopted him long after her. Cats are very territorial. He asserted himself with her when he came here to live and, given her nervous disposition, she reacted badly. So, she hides a lot. We're working on it. I spend extra quality time with her to diffuse the situation. She's not used to visitors either, so that may be a problem. Just keep Winklin away from her so she isn't upset. You can feed her separately upstairs. She has a favourite pink blankie on the brown lounger chair by the fireplace. Nice and cozy. Right, honey?" she crooned, stroking Nukkers tenderly. The cat's green eyes shot daggers at us.

"If you can't find her, look under this desk here. I think she feels safe behind the footstool. I put another one of her favourite pink, fuzzy blankies there too. Oh, I should mention that we did find her up in the third-floor attic once. We didn't show it to you when you were here. Its staircase is on the landing. It's a big old creepy room with hardly any light."

Lisa fluffed up the blanket. I swear Nukkers gave me the evil eye.

"I told Brad we don't have to use the attic. If we

need storage space, we can use the garage – and we have. I don't know how this little girl got past the door. Maybe a ghost let her in." She snickered and mugged a frightened face.

The cat wasn't impressed.

"I made Brad come up with me when I couldn't find her anywhere. He had to come home for lunch that day because I was so afraid. And there she was, curled up in a corner by the window. She actually had cobwebs hanging from her ears."

We followed her over to a brick counter. I couldn't help but feel some concern about Lisa's unbridled obsession with her cats' care.

"I start feeding them at 4:30." She showed us eight novelty kitty dishes on eight colourful kitty mats on the stone floor. They were bookended by automated blue water bowls.

I shot a quick look at Donna to see how she was taking this plethora of information. A bemused smile played over her face as she viewed our instructions covering the fridge door.

"Don't worry about the litter boxes. I just cleaned all nine and they will be fine until we come back tomorrow."

Thank God for small mercies. I wasn't going to worry.

Lisa nibbled at her thumbnail; her face suddenly sombre.

"I really appreciate this Mom. The place is still a mess and there's so much to do. I wanted you to see it when everything was arranged. I feel guilty for leaving. I'll have more time next week to organize. The editor is giving me a break from the cat newsletter. There's lots of food in the fridge and freezer. Please help yourselves."

She picked up a plastic baggie containing two small tins of wet food from a collection by the stove and held it up for us to see.

"All the diets for the next twenty-four hours are sorted into these and labelled with each cat's name. The pitchers of kibble are marked diet and regular. I fill the kibble bowls once per meal." She picked up a sample yellow bowl, bigger than the others, then looked at Donna. "You may confuse the tabbies. I know Mom still does."

She gave me a reproachful look.

"Anyway, their pastel portrait is in the living room if you need to check. Their names are under each face. Brad's friend created it. He also painted their faces on the mailbox by the road. He's so talented."

As Lisa walked away from us, she examined the living room, then returned to the kitchen island where we sat back on high swivel stools.

"Okay." She nodded to herself. "I think I've covered everything you need to know in a nutshell. If you have any questions, don't hesitate to call or text me." She stared at me. "I know you don't like texting, but it's the easiest way to communicate. My phone will be with me at all times."

She twisted an auburn lock of hair that had escaped from her curly ponytail. It was an old habit from childhood. Sometimes she still seemed like a little girl. I put my arm around her narrow shoulders and looked into her soft brown eyes.

"No worries. Your kitties are in good hands. Really, what's the worst that could happen in a matter of hours? It's not like you're flying off to the Caribbean like your neighbours. Your cats will be fed, watered, played with, and kept inside. You have covered all the bases with a great deal of information and printed prompts should our old, addled brains forget anything. Now off you go, and good luck with that presentation."

Donna stepped over and gave her a hug. "Don't you worry, hon." She stood back, assessing Lisa. "I will make sure your mom follows all your instructions to the letter."

We made our way out from the kitchen to the front

porch. No cats, not even Snappy, wove around our feet as Lisa closed the screen door softly. The bright glare of noon shimmered off Brad's SUV. He lounged back, enjoying the sun on his face.

"All set, Lise?" He turned to us with a smile. "Have fun ladies! Don't be afraid to make a dent in my temporary wine cellar. It's in the laundry room off the living room. There's lots of beer in the fridge too, if you prefer. Oh, and Reggie?"

He pointed to the two-car garage across from us.

"Lisa's Lexus is inside. The door opener has been unreliable. Seems to work when it feels like it. A handyman is coming Monday morning with a new set up. The remote is on the kitchen counter if you want to try getting it to open the door for your—"

"I won't be needing it. Not necessary. My car is fine under the trees." I motioned to the far side of the drive. "I mean, who's going to steal a car all the way out here?"

"Your car is safe." He laughed. "There's lots of four-legged critters around here, though. Thanks for this, ladies," Brad called, settling his bulky frame behind the steering wheel to start the engine. Lisa hoisted her leather bag onto her shoulder, then bent her head forward to climb into the passenger seat. She pulled back to look at me. Her forehead furrowed like something bothered her. This always reminded me of her father.

"I'm sure everything will be fine, Mom. Just please, please make sure they don't get out. That's really the only thing I'm worried about. They could get lost so easily in the forest out there." She waved at a wide treeline to the left of the house. "There are coyotes," she added, her warning ominous.

I put my two fingers up, like a Girl Guide.

"I promise, Lisa. We'll watch them just as we watched Kevin and you as little monsters. Now go and have some fun!" I waved her away with both hands to urge her on. Lisa gave a half-hearted smile and bent her head to climb in.

We watched their maroon Nissan SUV circle the drive, spinning a bit of dry gravel as they passed a grove of cedar trees. Lisa deserved a nice night out, I only hoped she didn't worry too much. This was my chance to show her she could rely on me.

CHAPTER THREE

Once they were out of sight, we wandered back to the house. Gold and crimson mid-autumn leaves danced over the stones in a soft gust of wind. I plunked myself with a loud moan onto a spindly wicker chaise. Donna propped herself against the porch railing, a perfect ad for Land's End catalogue in her navy pullover and crisp blue jeans. She looked dreamily over to a pond spilling lily pads. Tall bulrushes swayed over murky waters. An invisible bullfrog let out a guttural croak like a whoopee cushion.

"I don't think I would want all of this." She took in the view then looked at me and breathed deeply. "So much work. But it is peaceful out here. This stillness, being in the midst of nature would make it a marvelous bed and breakfast. A paradise for birdwatchers, artists, lovers…" Her voice trailed away as she studied her hands.

I agreed. "It would, but the guests would have to

be cat lovers. Hey, maybe there's a market for cat-fancier B&Bs. I was in a cafe in Yorkville a few years ago that had cats all over the place. Lazing over rafters, sleeping peacefully in fuzzy baskets, while customers quaffed coffee, wine, whatever."

"Sounds like what we have here."

I watched a filmy-winged dragonfly land on my Nike, but my mind was on my daughter.

"Lisa's okay with having *us* stay, but I don't think she could handle strangers in her home. She's private in so many ways. It's good that she has a freelancing job writing articles for *Canadian Cat Fancier*. She can keep the home fires burning and have no workplace stress. There are deadlines of course, but she's highly organized, always on top of her work. She's even given me a window of her availability should I choose to call her. I teased her about having OCD. She was offended." I sat back with a light laugh.

Donna chuckled. "Well, if being totally devoted to your cats is having OCD maybe she has it. Seriously though, I think people use that term way too much, myself included. Same with the word *anxiety*. Everyone talks about being anxious or stressed out. Speaking of stress, is Brad still doing the Toronto commute?"

Her words were followed by a scratching sound behind us. I looked over the back of the chaise to see Haylow, whom Lisa had previously described as the window-watcher tabby. She opened a wide pink mouth, and pressed her silver whiskers against the glass.

"Yes, he is, but it's closer from here. The LCBO offered him a new district manager position, so occasionally he works in Dunnville. All things considered, I would think they should be able to afford a handyman for next spring. As you said, there is so much to do."

I pushed myself up from the lounger with a gasp. My right knee was stiffer than usual. I gave it a soft rub.

"I need to stretch my legs. How about we go on a short exploration around the grounds before we make a dent in that temporary wine cellar?"

Donna brushed her hands together and followed me to the concrete and barn-board garage up ahead. Its double-car door was down. I wondered what the electrical glitch was that caused the trouble Brad had mentioned. Maybe it was just old and worn out, like my knee.

Conversely, the side garage door opened easily. We entered the cool, dank space, our eyes adjusting to the dim interior. A musty smell pervaded, reminding me of childhood-play in an old hayloft at my aunt and uncle's farm. Lisa's dusty black Lexus sat parked at the far wall. The garage could easily accommodate four vehicles. An impressive wall-to-wall, two-tiered workbench was built into the back of the room. A long bank of grimy windows along the wooden rafters filtered in the only sunlight.

"Hey! I've been in a dance hall this size." Donna's voice echoed through the dust motes in the still air.

"You mean Rick's Dance Hall at Morgan's Point, right?"

She nodded. "Yes. It wasn't The Cove, but I still liked going there once in a while. Shelly Arkin's grandmother had a cottage just down from Rick's. I stayed over a few times." She laughed. "Her Gramma was hard of hearing so the loud bands didn't keep her awake. And, Shelly had a key, so we could stay out as late as we liked."

"You young devils!" I leaned against the workbench. "You had it made. I only went once. Didn't have my licence back then. Who did I go with? God, I can't even remember. There was an awesome band that night. The joint was jumping to the song 'Land of A Thousand Dances.'"

"Wilson Pickett." Donna wiggled her hips dancing

around the room. I laughed, then joined her, waving my arms up and down, feet jiving in time to the beat as I shouted out the dances.

"Can you do the Pony? Or the Mashed Potato?"

Donna chimed in. "How about the Watusi, like little Lucy?"

Gradually, we weakened with laughter, trying to keep up with all the different moves as we dodged around crates and other obstacles in our path. I finally fell back against a stack of outdoor cushions, holding my chest while I gasped for air.

Donna stood at the far end of the room rummaging through some junk boxes. She cackled, then made her way still rockin' over to me. She held up an old table tennis paddle in each hand.

"I'll save you! Ready? Clear!" she shrieked, then went to slap them to my chest. I tried to push her away, helpless with the giggles. We clung to each other like a couple of Saturday night drunks. Standing, still laughing, I wiped moist mascara from my eyes.

"Oh my God!" I pressed a pain in my side. "You're crazier than me! Must be all this country air."

She leaned forward, hands on her knees, to catch her breath. "Nice to know we can still shake it, eh lady?" She gasped.

I nodded, pleased that my knee wasn't complaining for once. "You bet. Just set the party dates and I'll be there. Not sure how long on my feet though. Speaking of parties…"

I pointed out the monstrous Weber grill next to her. Brad was a diehard fan of bar-b-que. It was purchased a number of years before, but still looked new.

"Imagine the summer parties we could have out here. Pepper steak and lime-basted shrimp grilling, stereo blasting our music, tropical drinks flowing…" I looked over to a familiar glass patio table and eight sculpted iron chairs stacked in one corner.

"And neighbours not knowing." She snorted.

"Yeah. No complaints. Maybe remote country living has its perks."

"What are these for?" Donna's voice echoed behind me.

I turned to see her looking at a phalanx of rolled, black fencing, standing on end.

"That, my dear, is cat fencing." I gestured regally to the row. "It will be erected on the full perimeter of their backyard in the spring, if all goes according to their plan. They had it set up at their last place, but this area is five times that size, so they'll need to order more. Lisa's presentation tonight will be all about this recent invention that offers indoor cats outdoor safety."

We ran our hands over the smooth plastic-coated wire. It did seem quite strong.

"Gee. I thought I'd seen everything, Reggie." She spied the far end of the fencing. "So, it curves over at the top to keep them in should they try to escape?"

"That's the idea, and it's a lot cheaper than electric fencing." I raised my eyebrows and talked out of the side of my mouth with a wicked grin like Groucho Marx.

"Go on!" she scoffed. "I hope you didn't say that to Lisa!"

I headed back to the entrance. "For your ears only. You understand my dark humour," I whispered dramatically, clicking the heavy door shut behind us.

An ancient, plank potting shed clung like a barnacle to the far side of the garage. I dodged around a rusted-out plough to a small web-festooned window and peered in, not wanting to touch anything.

"Any corpses?" Donna called out.

"I can't see any. Pretty dirty though. Here, I'll try to open the door."

I pressed the flaking latch down and pushed carefully with my hip. The timber squealed in protest, as the door creaked inward. There was just enough space for me to poke my head in and take a quick look around.

"Nothing interesting," I called back to her, "Just a rusted-out push mower and lots of cobwebs." I bent my head for an abrupt sneeze. "Dust and old hay. Just what my sinuses need." Grasping the latch, I gave a hard yank and the door closed.

We meandered through waist-high grasses to another pond, this one smaller and more overgrown than the first. Insects buzzed around our heads in the warm afternoon light.

"Hey, Donna, how are Kev and Leo doing?" We pushed through stalks of goldenrod and proud stands of purple phlox along the water. Her son and his partner tended to keep to themselves.

"Quite well, actually. Kevin has a good chance of securing a sabbatical to work on his thesis and Leo has had some amazing success with his investment firm. He's attracted a lot of interest from California celebrities."

My radar perked up. "Any big ones?" I ventured, feeling a thrill. She picked a stubborn burr from her jeans then looked over at me.

"How about George Clooney or Keanu Reeve?" She shot up her eyebrows and broke into a wide grin.

"What? No way. I mean, he hangs out with them?"

She shrugged. "I think most of the business is

handled through clients' accountants. I'll have to ask him if he's actually met them. Do you want an autograph? Would that float your boat? Do you still have Bobby Curtola's?" she teased.

I slapped a hand to my forehead. "It was hard work getting Bobby's autograph in '66. I had to fight off goofy, wailing, teenage girls, then get in an argument with a pompous floorwalker who was an absolute toad! I waited two damn hours for my chance to touch my idol's shirtsleeve in Kresge's storefront window!"

I idly started to hum "Fortune Teller" as I followed Donna's swaying blue sweater through the grasses to the trimmed yard.

My friend came to a standstill, letting me catch up to her. She linked her arm with mine and let out a soft sigh.

"You know, I'm really happy for Kevin and Leo. I have to admit, it was hard for Jim and I to accept Kevin's coming out.

"Really?" She nodded at my shocked expression and grimaced, her lips drawing a tight line.

"Yes. I didn't tell you at the time, but I was ashamed about what I felt was a dreadful secret." She huffed out a sigh, lowering her eyes to study her wide, gold wedding band.

"I'll never forget the night he told us. I was sitting on the sofa in the living room with the evening newspaper. It was a Friday night. The TV was on. The theme song from *Jeopardy* played. Jim made some comment about gas prices rising again when Kevin walked into the room. He had a strange uneasiness about him. You know what a kidder he is, but there was no smile this time." Donna's eyes lost focus, looking into the past.

"He was wearing a red Polo shirt with white cargo pants and I remember being struck by how clean-cut and good looking he was."

I stopped by a smooth granite rock and studied her face. She had never opened up this way before.

"He said he didn't want to hurt us, but we needed to know he was gay. That he had only dated a few girls so he could make it through high school without a big hassle. He wanted top marks to get into McGill. He wasn't active, because he was waiting for the right guy."

Donna sat on the rock, her gaze on a rustic bridge over the pond.

"I crushed the newspaper into my lap and burst into sobs. I couldn't believe it. I didn't want to. Jim had a worried frown when he looked at me. Kevin stood like a lonely stranger staring at the two of us.

After what seemed like hours, Jim breathed out a sigh. I watched him go to our boy and take him into his arms. Kevin cried into his neck, then pulled his head up to watch my face. Jim turned and held out his arm to me."

Donna bent her head to twist her wedding ring.

"'Come here, Mother,' he'd said softly. I shook my head in disbelief. Our son. Our only child. But something inside me, some maternal instinct, got me up from the sofa and I went to them. I knew I'd always love my son, but the news was hard to take. I felt shame and betrayal, then later guilt for my feelings. It took us a few years to fully come to terms with it. But I see now that Kevin and Leo make such a well-suited couple. They are always there for each other, and they have been so kind and caring to me, especially since…" Her blue eyes filled and I moved over to hold her.

It occurred to me that I'd never thought to delve deeper into her admission about Kevin years back. I was glad she finally opened up to me.

"Hey, it's okay, Donna. Go ahead. Let it out. Remember, Jim will always be with you."

I hugged her drooping shoulders as she quietly wept. After a moment she pulled back and gave me a sad smile, then wiped at her eyes with long fingers.

"I try to be busy, you know, to keep the hours filled." She sniffed and reached into her jeans pocket for a tissue. We took our time heading toward the back deck. I paused and looked up at a startling, cerulean sky. She followed my gaze, a pale hand shielding her eyes.

"I know you do"—I turned to her—"but you're still working through a big change. There's no timeline on grief, honey."

She nodded. "Oh, I know that. But these moments just come out of the blue, like the quiet of night when sleep won't come, and I reach out to an empty sheet. Or when something wonderful happens and I want to share my excitement with him."

She tucked a loose strand of flaxen hair behind her ear. We stepped up on the wide cedar of the deck, smoothing our jeans to sit and take in nature's vista. A magnificent blue heron cut the stillness, soaring across our view like a dark pterodactyl. It landed on some outcropping at the edge of the creek. Donna touched my hand and dropped her voice.

"It's the loneliness, Reggie. That's what gets to me. It comes when I least expect it. I can be busy in a crowd of people, involved in various activities, like club functions, volunteering, travelling, when all of a sudden, I feel the pang of emptiness." She eyed my

37

expressionless face. Donna lonely? With her busy life? I didn't know what to say.

"Don't you ever get lonely, Reggie? You've been on your own for years and I've never heard you complain about it. You're so independent. I guess it didn't occur to me, but don't you find it painful at times?"

Her wide eyes searched mine. A wave of gloom washed over me. I hadn't really thought about loneliness. I pulled out a stringy dandelion that had stubbornly pushed through the decking and absently played with it.

"I can't compare my situation to yours, Donna. Your marriage to Jim was an inspiration to all who knew you. A match made in heaven, as the saying goes. I didn't get that with Sam. We really weren't good together. My Irish temper and his roving eye. It was so hard with work, looking after a baby, him gone most of the time."

I frowned at my recollection.

"He had his work, then the guys after work. I was alone, for the most part, whether he was there or not. So, when I finally left him, I didn't look back. I was used to my own company, raising our child. He soured me on men in general, and the few dates I've had since our split, just reinforced that dis-

JUDITH READ

appointment. You know…" I paused, looking for my own consolation, rubbing the limp plant between my fingers. "I've become very routine-based since retiring from the library. There always seems to be something to do. I love early-morning time at the gym, coffee chats with old friends. I'm even thinking about doing some daily journaling. And I read more than ever! I get lost in some character's life and vicariously adventure through them." I smiled, thinking about my latest psychological thriller.

"Once I get into a story that grabs me from the first page, I'm gone. I lose track of time. I can't wait to get back to the story. A few years ago, I ditched a date with a guy to return to my reading."

She looked stunned. A part of me wanted to laugh, not at her but myself.

"Maybe books are my antidote to loneliness. A distraction. Just like people who watch T.V. or spend a lot of time online," I admitted, "you say I'm so independent, and I do like being that way, but I'm glad I have friends I can count on, like you."

Rising from the step, I threw the weed away and rubbed my hands together. "Well, I think this is the time where I say, hey, how about a drink?"

She stretched her long arms skyward, wiggled her fingers and slowly rose from the step.

"And I say bring it on, sister!"

As we crossed over to the French doors, Winky carefully observed our movements through the window. He mouthed a wide yowl and brushed against the door, his long orange and white plumed tail waved like a flag.

"And for God's sake, Donna, make sure that old evil eye there doesn't escape. Looks like he's just sizing up an opportunity to make a run for it!"

—o0o—

CHAPTER FOUR

"**D**an, it's a job interview. Worn-out running shoes aren't gonna cut it."

Dan watched Jessica's lovely mouth twisted into a sneer as she glared at his feet. She was in her habitual "hurry-up mode." He'd grabbed his stuff recklessly to keep up. They stood face to face in the faux-Greek revival lobby of her upscale apartment building.

He swept his hair out of his eyes then looked down at his favourite blue Keds. *Okay, they're old, but who cares?* He had hoped she wouldn't notice, but then again, there wasn't much she missed.

"I'm really not into this, Jess. I'm not a salesman. I'm a musician and there's a big difference." He let out a deep sigh, surveying his feet.

"You got that right. One makes money and the other doesn't." She stormed out the door in a huff to her leased BMW, clutching her favourite Prada bag.

"All right, all right," he muttered to himself and

turned to go back inside to find other shoes.

"Never mind. We're going to be late. Hopefully, the interviewer won't look at your feet."

She glared as he grappled with the passenger door like it was a ten-ton weight. "What's in that backpack? You can't take that to a job interview." Leaning over, she grabbed the bag from his hand and threw it into the back seat.

"Just stop. I know what I'm doing."

"My father went to a lot of trouble for you to have this chance. Don't blow it." She flounced into the driver's seat.

Fifteen minutes later the car roared to a stop at Larson and Associates Insurance Brokerage, just missing the curb. Dan stared forlornly at the three-story, dull brick building. Totally unimaginative in design, it reminded him of a medical arts building from the sixties. *This feels like a trip to the dentist… for a root canal.* He wanted to jump out of the car and run like hell. Anywhere but here.

The silver bangles on Jessica's arm jangled as she turned to him, her piercing, gray eyes all business. "Text me when you're done. Where's your resume and cover letter? References?" she barked like a drill sergeant. He flung up a business folder, putting his hand on the door to get out of the car.

She clutched his arm to pull him back to her. "Not so fast, Loverboy." She softened and offered him full, pink lips. He bent his head for a quick kiss, then ducked out and slammed the door.

As she peeled away, he remained transfixed, watching her gun the Beemer into downtown traffic. He pulled out his phone from the suit jacket pocket. There was plenty of time… to wait.

He ambled over to a parkette by the insurance building. Maybe it just came down to his mood. Lately, he'd been feeling like crap and it wouldn't take much to set him off.

He dropped down onto a dull, iron bench and slouched back to get comfortable. With his middle finger, he pushed up his Armani shades, a birthday gift from Jess, and glanced at the job folder lying beside him.

He wriggled around on the hard bench, which might as well have been concrete under his skinny butt. The suit felt all wrong after sloppy T-shirts and blue jeans. Dan stuck his finger under the tight Oxford collar and tugged. He watched a couple of teenagers in dreadlocks throw a purple frisbee by a small grove of trees. Their dog, one of those yappy Jack Russell mutts, bounced back and forth trying to catch it.

His mind wandered back to when he first met Jess.

43

A muggy summer evening. He'd decided to treat himself to an Iced Capp at Tim Hortons before practice.

She sat alone in a corner, a sheaf of wheat-coloured hair hanging over her eyes. Something made him move in her direction. It was like his feet had developed a mind of their own. When she looked up, he was startled. In spite of her tear-streaked face and runny mascara, she was the most beautiful woman he'd ever seen.

"I was so stupid!" she spat the words out. "It was over money. Money! Now my sister's gone. Dead! Three years of not speaking to her. I was so stubborn and stupid."

Her confession made him uncomfortable. He paused for a moment, then whispered. "That's really terrible. I'm sorry for invading your space. You looked lonely and I thought – well, never mind. You probably want to be alone."

"Thank you. You're nice to say that. Actually, sometimes it helps to have someone who will listen, even a stranger. I need to get out of here. Do you want to go for a walk?"

That was over a year ago. It was a tough time for her. She was estranged from her older sister, Taylor, over an inheritance. She died in a car crash in Alberta.

Jess's mom gave her a hard time because of the sisters' estrangement, as if Jess didn't feel guilty enough. Dan figured her old man probably didn't help the dysfunction, as Jess was obviously his favourite daughter.

Dan had made a lot of allowances for her demands because of her past, but his patience was wearing thin.

Let's get Dan a job, whether he wants it or not, became a family mantra. He wasn't stupid. He knew he had to get something. The gigs were unreliable. The band needed regular bookings and venues they could depend upon for cash flow. It didn't help that their lead singer had a drinking problem. He was becoming more erratic than ever. Jake, on lead guitar, was doing okay. He had a steady day job as a welder.

Dan knew he looked like a street bum in the shadow of Jess's style. His friends told him she was a snob and he could do a lot better. He was proud of her, though. She'd taken business administration in college and graduated top of her class. This got her financing manager at one of the top import car dealerships in the region. Maybe, in some weird way, he loved her. He kind of got a kick out of the head-turns she scored from other guys. She was hot, no question.

But her nagging was the same old shit.

Then an opportunity from a friend of her *dear old dad* came up. Dan would qualify to sell life insurance after taking an eight-week course in customer relations. Easy money, her father assured him, because it was an established clientele.

The bench seemed harder. Even the loose pants stuck to him. It had to be thirty degrees out here. The monkey suit didn't help.

A sick dread filled Dan's stomach as he stood up next to the bus shelter. He clutched his business folder tighter while he read the gaudy ad for Ms. Phaedra's Card Readings on the wall next to him. Maybe that's what he needed right now, some insight as to how the interview for the job he didn't want was going to go.

The tie Jess Windsor-knotted so carefully for him noosed his neck. His fingers pulled at the shirt collar as he twisted his head to find comfort.

A bus slid over to the shelter with a squeal and a hiss. The logo for Jack's Town Tavern emblazoned the side of it. That's where he'd rather be. What a great gig they'd had there two weeks ago. The bar crowd had banged their drinks and hollered for more. His long fingers mimed a riff on his hip, as he thought about it. Too bad he wasn't here for an audition.

He sighed, then turned back to look again at the plain brick facade of the four-storey building before him.

Time to get going and stop over thinking. Dan pushed open the double-plate glass doors. He walked over to a wide mahogany reception desk and waited, tapping a beat on the floor with his toe. A middle-aged woman in a red power suit and tight French twist took his name and made a quick call. He swallowed and watched the buzz around him. Lots of suits and well-cut hair. People who were all business.

"They're expecting you. Head on up to the third floor." The receptionist then dutifully ignored him.

"Thanks." Dan moved away, joining the people waiting for the doors to open. He caught a glance of himself in the mirrored wall; borrowed suit, tight tie, and a stressed look. He didn't need a psychic reading to tell him his future. Dan made a beeline for the washroom.

—o0o—

CHAPTER FIVE

"Do you believe in that Tarot stuff?" Donna asked, staring at the portrait of the cats – their nine faces gazing back at us.

I had just ended an unexpected call with Persia, my cousin. Mulling over Donna's question, I snapped a picture of the portrait and read the names printed below each kitty: Montana, Nukkers, Winklin, Snappy, Joey, Hermie, Haylow, Sarge, and Spruce. We walked over to our wine, an air of expectation hovering between us. I picked up my glass, pausing in midair before sipping.

"I find it entertaining, but I wouldn't run my life according to a pack of cards." Guilt gnawed at me for forgetting Persia's invitation to a vegan lunch date today. I gave Donna a critical look. She'd said she was okay with me inviting Persia over, yet I had to wonder.

I shrugged. "That's just me, and you know how cynical I am. I suppose it's like anything else that people become addicted to. A quick fix, like, *What will my day be like? Will I get that job promotion? Will I meet Mr. Right? Should I get a boob job? Let's see what the cards say!* Persia believes in those future predictions. She always has. Her gift lies in revelations to others. She makes her own consultations about everyday stuff; whether or not to go certain places, if she should make a financial investment, medical decisions, even her love life."

"Maybe that's a good thing," Donna mused, reaching past me to pick up her own glass. "I mean, to have confidence in that kind of guidance."

I chuckled. "Well, she sure has that. Persia thinks the world would be a more peaceful place if we could all find our spiritual paths. I'm going to—" A blood curdling wail cut me off. Donna and I jumped as tiny Nukkers tore past us engaged in a scrap with her nemesis, one-eyed Winky. We raced up stairs in search of the two. Donna checked the spare room while I ducked into the master bedroom and spotted Nukkers high up on one of the climbers – Winky nowhere in sight.

I leaned around the doorframe back into the hall. "I found her."

Donna popped out of the other room and joined me. We stared at the little kitty, letting her calm down a moment.

"I take it Persia has returned from the ashram in India?"

"Oh, she's been to other places since then. I believe Tuscany was her last destination."

Nukkers rubbed her face into the carpeted stand and licked a paw. That was my cue. I picked her up. Donna followed us downstairs and I laid her, peacefully, in a purple woven cat basket above our heads in the living room.

Two more gray tigers slept in the climbers by the windows, arms splayed over the sides. I made a mental note to double-check their portrait. So far, I could only recognize three.

"Persia's treating us to dinner. Could be interesting."

"You said she was vegan."

"Yeah, she's a little out there, but there's never a dull moment with Persia around."

Donna's lips twitched, amused. "I do love her name. Is that her real name? It's so unusual."

I called up the picture I took of the kitty portrait – no mean feat as technology was my nemesis – and examined the tabbies' framed faces before answering.

"No. She was plain old Sharon until she went to California back in the seventies. You remember her, right?"

Donna turned her blond head to the side thinking, and curled her long legs up on the couch.

"Yes. I saw her at a craft show in Thorold a couple of years ago. She was doing rock readings. Beautiful silk drapes cascaded from the ceiling of her tent. Lots of tie-dyed and hemp clothing. There was a childlike sweetness about her. I stood by the entrance to watch and found myself mesmerized by her interactions with customers. They seemed to be as taken with her gentleness as I was.

"You first introduced us at Lisa and Brad's engagement party. She's very pretty in a boho way. That long, wavy nimbus of hair and those masses of beads and scarves."

I smiled at Donna's description of my skinny younger cousin who'd never left the sixties.

"You know, she was always a bit different. Kind of innocent, small for her age, big watery-blue eyes. Some of our family thought she was strange. She seemed to prefer the company of creatures to humans when she was growing up. She played in a treehouse and took most of her meals up there until she was starting junior high. Mom said she was just very young for her age.

"I lost track of her for a while. She lived in Southern California for years when I was busy with work and motherhood. She never married or lived with anyone I knew of – insisted that destiny would provide her soul mate if she required one, and in its own sweet time."

A meow came from behind me. Winklin gave me the eye. *There you are, you little rabble rouser.*

"I should look around and see where all the other cats are, so when Lisa texts, I'll have my report ready, to ease her worried mind."

I set my phone down, stood up, and ran a hand through my unruly, short curls, a curse from my maternal grandmother. It seemed like a good idea to check where all our charges were and do the cat count as per our instructions. Actually, I didn't mind that much. The staircase exercise might be good for me. If my knee told me otherwise, I'd send Donna to check on them.

She pointed under Brad's desk. "Don't forget Spruce, or is it Sarge? I can't tell those two apart. Big, gray tabbies. Both cuties."

"I know what you mean." I stared at two more cats on the counter. "Okay, I count five tabs, and Winky down here. I'll just go up and see if the other three are roaming around in the bedrooms."

At the top of the stairs, I stood to admire the second floor, now that I wasn't in a rush to rescue

Nukkers. So much room. A large fieldstone fireplace took up one orange brick wall in the bright open den, banked by two ornate stained-glass windows. Sunlight streamed onto the polished floor in hues of deep crimson, forest green and royal blue. On the other side of the open staircase, a wide hallway ran with doors opening to four bedrooms. Boxes lined the hall, waiting to be distributed. I peeked into the master bedroom.

Sweet old Montana, the three-legged guy, lay curled in a tight ball off to dreamland on the king-sized bed. To the right, stretched out on the triple dresser, was the black and white Snappy. I reached to gently stroke his fur. A loud *thwack* from downstairs startled both of us. His eyes jerked awake, senses on high alert.

Donna's cry echoed up the staircase.

"Oh, God! Reggie, come here!" she shrieked.

I swung away from the bedroom, almost wiping out on the stair bannister, and raced down.

"Something hit the window. Like a gunshot!" She pointed toward the deck, eyes bugged wide. I inched closer. No obvious damage to the glass, and I couldn't see what had scared her so much.

"What is…?" I started to ask, then crept gingerly to the window for a better look. Maybe some hunter had shot an animal out there. I shivered at the thought and bent my head forward to scan the deck. A huge blackbird, iridescent feathers gleaming in the sun, lay still under the window.

I recalled my mother's old superstition. Apparently, the bird's passing foretold of a coming death. I recoiled at the thought of disposing of its giant body just as the bird wobbled, shook its head, then soared into the distant trees. I was relieved, not only for the bird but by a respite from possible ill luck. Shaking my head, I walked over and gave Donna's shoulder a playful squeeze.

"Geez, you scared me. I heard something hit the house. I didn't even think of a bird. Damn, it was big."

She shivered, then gasped. "Eww, I'm glad it flew away. You would've had to take care of its body, I'm too chicken. No pun intended."

With a deep gust of breath, she sagged into the couch. "It's so quiet here. You don't expect sudden noise. Guess I'm just a soft city slicker. Can you imagine what pioneer life was like in the old days? I wonder how we would survive all the scary stuff."

I scratched my head to think.

"Pioneers were a different breed for sure. Tough, with stamina. If we didn't know any differently, we might be all right. Laundry would be a bitch." I grinned.

She laughed; her good humour restored. I considered how easy it was to take things for granted. "But with all we have now, it's hard to imagine. This crazy, high-tech world we live in. Just think of life today if there was a massive power outage and people couldn't charge their phones? Total chaos. I heard a young teen in Walmart moan to her friend in the check-out line that she would just die without her phone."

"Oh, I've heard similar, and it's not just the kids. All ages glued to their phones. I admit to using my own a lot sometimes. It's just so handy."

Pausing, she studied her manicured nails, head tilted to the side.

"Did you know, Reggie, there are places people seek to get away from online addictions?"

"Nothing surprises me." I took a long sip of Brad's Chateau Merlot 2012. It was very satisfying.

"Places of meditation," she went on, "like monasteries. Remember Jacinthe, our aerobics teacher from a few years back? Her daughter Holly went to Plum Village in France to get away from her cell phone and into the teachings of Thich Nhat Hanh, the Vietnamese Zen Master. There's an old Buddhist monastery there that offers retreats for Westerners to escape the hectic, stress-filled North American way of life."

I looked over at her and watched her intense expression with amusement.

"And how did Holly like hanging with the monks instead of hanging off her phone?"

Donna threw her hands up to the ceiling in a mime of frustration.

"She only lasted two days. It was supposed to be a week. She hopped a train to Paris, ran amok, shopped her head off, then flew back to her phone."

I clapped my hands, and rocked forward on the couch, chuckling. "Speaking of phones, I should check mine. I know Lisa will have texted."

I made my way past a train of empty boxes to the kitchen. Sure enough, there was a message from my daughter wanting to know if the cats were adjusting to us. I smiled and replied that we were all getting on like a house on fire, then changed that to simply say we were fine. No sense alarming her. She got right back to me, relieved when I told her that the cats were okay.

"All is well, Donna." I returned to my favourite retro chair. "They are settled in at the Westin. I hope she can rest easy in the knowledge that her cats are safe with us and we can relax with a wine refresher and some good jazz." I passed her the bottle from the coffee table and headed over to the stereo to check out their CD collection.

"What happened to this poor guy's leg?" Donna called from the living room. I pivoted around to see her stroking Montana, who writhed luxuriously under her gentle touch.

"He was caught in a leg-hold trap," I said absently, my attention back on the music. She spoke softly to him and scooped him up carefully. He snuggled into her shoulder, purring.

"He was one of their first rescues, six years ago. He and Winky are Lisa's favourites I'd say." I watched her cuddle Montana a moment longer, then went back to my CD quest. I chose an Art Pepper tucked in a stereo rack; glad the kids had unpacked it.

"When's Persia coming?" she asked.

I paused by the stereo and shrugged. "My cousin is no slave to the clock. Could be anytime this afternoon. Hopefully by dinner. I can't wait for a kale and lentil feast or whatever it is she's concocted."

She cackled, then moved to put Montana back down on the sofa. "Would it be rude to use a back-up meal from the well-stocked fridge?"

"Oh, you mean like a juicy T-bone steak with nonorganic vegetables?" I teased. The smooth beat of classic jazz filled the air. A soft thump came from the kitchen. Winklin prowled the line up of empty cat food dishes. I laughed at the busy boy.

"Looks like we're getting told it's chow time. Come on, Donna. Help me figure out who's who for what dish. Do you think they'll notice if we goof up?"

"Well they can't tell their folks, can they?" she raised an eyebrow conspiratorially.

I snickered when it struck me that they couldn't. The clatter of cutlery and bowls alerted the other cats. In no time, they appeared from all over the house and swarmed into the kitchen. There were eight moving felines, but no Nukkers. Then I remembered the small cat's fear of Winky and Lisa's directive. I would feed her separately.

"Grab your spoon, food bag, and designated cat." I grabbed mine. "Trying not to trip over them will be the hard part."

"It's a feeding frenzy!" she exclaimed.

—oOo—

CHAPTER SIX

Dan stared out the window as Jessica's midnight blue ride wove its way recklessly through mid-afternoon traffic. For once, he didn't care how badly she drove. Maybe she'd crash her car and he could escape the coming shitstorm. He gnawed at a hangnail on his thumb.

"Did you hear me? Dan? Are you sick? Where's the suit? I know you were nervous about the interview, but it went well, didn't it?" She glanced away from the road, her stern look probing his.

He went back to his window. "I'm tired. The suit was too hot. I changed in the washroom. That's all, no big deal. It went okay. The guy was cool."

She whooshed her breath out in relief. "Oh, good then. Was it Tony? The interviewer?" she chirped. "Daddy just thinks he's amazing. He's one of their top salespeople and would be a wonderful mentor for you. I mean we all have to start somewhere. You just didn't get a good start that's all." She swerved sharply, cutting off a burly, grizzled biker on a Harley.

Dan clutched the door handle, squeezing hard. "Hey, easy!" His heart hammered his chest.

She laughed off his fear and waved a flirty hand at the poor bastard behind them. Dan turned his head in time to see the biker scowl and flip her the bird. She tilted her head to adjust her sunglasses and nonchalantly check her lipstick in the rear-view mirror. Satisfied, she turned to Dan.

"This may be premature, hon, but I want to celebrate your new beginning."

He darted another quick look at her. Daddy's girl was revving up, he could feel it. It was a crappy feeling.

"You'll get the job, don't worry." She breathed out blissfully, then moved into a trademark rapid-monologue. "It's pretty much a done deal. You're smart. You'll breeze through the sales course with flying colours. And I have to admit you looked hot in that suit. Now, all we have to do is get you a couple of designer suits of your own, and some button-down shirts, of course, snappy ties too. Personally, I like Brooks Brothers, but we'll go on a shopping expedition, maybe one of the outlet malls to start. Don't worry, you can take your time paying me back. It'll be so great to see you dressing for success. Makes all the difference, you'll see. I can take you to work until you get your car fixed, maybe you could eventually upgrade to something newer." She checked her lip gloss again.

He made another side-eye. She looked far too pleased with herself, almost serene, which was pretty good for her. But then, she was in the driver's seat. Jess slapped his arm, startling him from his thoughts.

"Hey you, wake up!" she shouted. "We're going for a surprise! My treat. I hope you're hungry. You didn't look so good when I picked you up." She gave a giggle and squeezed his thigh. For once his manhood didn't react.

"I actually thought you may have blown off the interview." She looked back to the mirror.

He gritted his teeth and dug his nails into sweating palms as she plowed on.

"Silly of me really. My father went to great lengths to get this set up and I know you'd never let him down. Or me." She finally stopped her chatter to search the turn up ahead.

"This looks like the road. Almost there. Aren't you excited?"

Jess took a sudden turn off the main thoroughfare. He grabbed the door handle battling a strong desire to eject himself from the vehicle.

"Dan? Danny? What's up with you? Look out your window at all the grapevines! Now, do you know where we're headed?" She leaned into him playfully; her hot breath bathed the side of his neck.

"Where are we going?" His head was starting a slow, dull throb.

She jerked back to her steering wheel with an exaggerated sigh.

"Okay, okay, I'll give you another clue. I hope you're in the mood for wine." She flashed him a flirty wink, batting her eyelashes. His gaze cut to her thigh, smooth tanned skin peeking out from a sexy pink mini dress.

They passed through vast tilled acreages punctuated by deep woods. He gave her a weak smile. "Yeah, I could use some alcohol right now."

"Sheila, at work, has been telling me about this winery for ages and I am so pumped for it. Oops. I gave it away, sorry! But you know me. I'm not good at keeping secrets. I do love celebrations. And private ones afterward." She gave him a sly wink, then pooched out a full pink lip.

"Shouldn't be much further, maybe I should've used the GPS, but I wanted to make it a surprise." Her oversized Ray-Bans, perched on her turned-up nose, scanned the side of the road. "There should be a sign for Elite Vintages, then a long driveway."

Dan squirmed uncomfortably, like he was going to piss himself. He couldn't hold back any longer.

"Jess, look. I have to tell you…" He clenched his hands together on his lap. It was now or never.

"I didn't think it would be this far out," she interrupted, her eyes diverted to the side of the road. "Sorry, you were saying something?"

She was still distracted, but Dan went for it anyway. "I'm not taking the job."

Jess leaned over the steering column and turned her blonde head back to the road. "Shoot! I wonder if I missed it back there? I'm just going to go ahead a bit more before I turn around."

She floored the accelerator then shot him a look.

"I didn't hear you. You were muttering something about the job?"

"I didn't take the job. I don't want it!" An immense relief rushed through him like a burst abscess.

The car ground to a death-defying halt. His head snapped back, one elbow smashing the door handle. Dust billowed around the windows.

"What?" she screamed; her face flushed with sudden rage. A pretty woman turned ugly.

"You heard me. You don't listen to me though!"

63

In one livid movement, she jerked the car's shifter into park.

"Did you even go to the interview?" She tore off her sunglasses and ran a frantic hand through dishevelled hair.

"It went okay. I went!" he hollered, recoiling against the car door. "The guy, Tony, he liked me, okay? We talked a lot. Just not about insurance training programs."

"Then… what the hell did you talk about?" she bit off each word through bared teeth.

He heaved an agonized hiss and looked away from her to stare straight ahead.

"Music. We talked about music. The guy admires talented local musicians. He said he knew by my whole-body language when I sat down that I would never sell insurance policies. He told me to do what makes me happy and what I was good at. He read some magazine article about doing what you love. That it's a healthier way to live. Told me I'm young enough to suck it up and go for it. He's right. I liked him."

"Oh, that makes it all better," she mocked. "You liked him. How sweet."

Her knuckles shone white in contrast to the black steering wheel. A dead silence hovered between them, save for his breathing.

"Get out!" She stared straight ahead and spat the two words like a curse.

He gingerly touched her bare arm. "Just calm down and listen, Jess." His whispered words were urgent. She slapped his hand away and pushed him hard into the passenger door. He'd never seen her so pissed off.

"Get out of my car, loser!" She shook her fist at him.

He scrambled to break free of the seatbelt, his usually quick hands fumbling with the catch. As he took the handle, the car door flew open and he landed face down on the gravel shoulder. The Beemer jerked into drive with a sickening grind. He looked up in time to see it tear away in a cloud of dust.

He was still coughing on exhaust fumes when the car skidded to a squealing stop further up the road. His eyes stung as he watched Jessica clamber out from the driver's side and pitch something hard into the deep brush along the ditch.

"Here's your phone, Dan!" she shouted back, her voice dripping with rage. "Don't ever think of calling me. You're nothing but a selfish, self-centred jerk. A waste of space. You'll never amount to anything!"

The Beemer blew away in an angry cloud of gravel and dust.

—o0o—

CHAPTER SEVEN

Persia Orly travelled serenely in her tangerine Volkswagen van along a pleasant country road that reminded her of a John Constable landscape. She smiled at the sustainable gifts of nature; wide views of fertile fields interwoven with a palette of forest hues. What a fine autumn day to treasure while rolling along in her four-wheeled sanctuary.

The van was a second home away from her small loft apartment in Binbrook. It carried all she held dear; the much-loved Gibson guitar a former flame had gifted to her, an array of silk window dressings she created herself, books by favourite authors; Kahlil Gibran, Jack Kornfield, Thomas Moore, the Dalai Lama, that she had collected over the years.

A carpenter friend had built-in little oak drawers to hold her crystals, reading rocks, runes and Tarot cards. Her pride and joy was a stunning shag rug, boasting purple, mustard and indigo hues that graced the floor of her spirit traveller, as she liked to call the van.

She glided along, at peace, humming to her favourite Ravi Shankar CD, feeling incredibly at one with birdsong and azure sky, when she spotted a lone figure up ahead. He hunkered down by the ditch at the side of the road.

She peered over her wire rims to make out a young man, possibly twenty something, in a dejected state of being. He may have been hurt or homeless. She slowed the van to pull it carefully off the road. The motor's hum got his attention. His handsome, tanned face gazed up at her as if he woke from a trance. She hoisted herself over to the passenger side for a closer look.

"Excuse me? Do you need help?" she asked, her voice high, one bony hand clutching the window frame.

He raised himself with some effort, straightened his leather belt, and brushed the road dirt off his jeans.

"That's debatable." he grunted, pushing back a lock of dirty blond hair with a smooth hand. He pointed to the van. "Cool ride. Looks like a '72."

"You know your cars." She grinned, flashing large even teeth. "May I give you a lift somewhere?"

He paused, holding a hand over his brow to take in her gauzy hippie dress and long gray pigtails.

He waved vaguely in the direction of the woods

ahead. "My phone is in the bush there somewhere."

She wrinkled her long nose and peered up the road. A rattling feed truck broke the silence as it lumbered past. She craned her neck to frown at the driver's dust, then returned to the young man.

"Were you hiking out here? Where did you park your car?" She stared at something above his head and he turned to look. Nothing there.

"It's a long story, ma'am. I won't go into it." His teeth wrestled his bottom lip and he dropped his head.

She considered. There was definitely something to be done here, but it would take time. She closed her eyes and held her sacred bloodstone pendant in her dominant right hand, then hummed in a low tone. When the sound faded out and she opened her eyes, he watched her, bewildered. That was nothing new, she'd been stared at a lot in sixty-two years.

"My name is Persia." She held out her hand to take his warm one off the van window and rubbed it gently, then announced, "You are in a very negative place at this time. I can sense your pain. And it comes from here." She held her bejewelled, tapered fingers to her heart. He stood immobilized as her eyes searched his face with an unblinking blue gaze.

"I see a gray aura around you. Do you know what an aura tells?"

He shook his head, eyes still vigilant.

"An aura is an energy field that can make itself known around a person's body. It flows in one or more colours. Aural energy cannot be seen by everyone, but you don't have to be in the spiritual realm to see it. Often, it's quite beautiful. Yours isn't. Not to offend, but I'm getting unhappiness from yours."

He wiped his face with the back of his hand when she pressed her fingers to his for a brief moment. Her hand was as cool and soft as sand.

"What is your name?" she asked.

He raised his eyebrows, gave a speculative look, then answered.

"Dan Riverton."

In one swift movement, she threw open the van door and beckoned him in. He shrugged, then wiped his hands on his jeans and pulled himself in beside her.

"Well, Dan Riverton," she said, as he struggled with the ancient seat belt. "Maybe a bit of diversion would be good for your soul. Unless you have other plans, which something tells me you don't. If at any point you wish me to drive you home, I will gladly do so. As you may have noticed, I am sensitive to the spiritual world." She pointed a long finger to the back of the van. He glanced to the rear and took in marked import boxes of candles, incense holders, essences and crystals.

"Hey, you're like a fortune teller or something?" he asked.

She shot him a quick look, then shifted the van into drive.

"We're on our way. Adventure awaits. I can feel it!" she cried. A pale, multifaceted amethyst necklace swung like a pendulum from the rear-view mirror.

"In a manner of speaking. I am a fortune-teller. I do feel that's a rather old-fashioned term, and I don't like its connotation of swindling the innocent. I prefer the term psychic or spirit traveller. And I don't use a crystal ball. Too hokey." She trilled a high musical laugh. He sat back on his quilted seat to watch her.

"I'm bringing a special vegan dinner I created to my cousin and her friend. They're not vegan, but they may convert after they taste the spread I've brought!" she grinned. Her fingers smoothed back a strand of silver hair the wind had blown across her high forehead.

"It's not much further up the road, I think. A big, old country place. They're looking after it while her daughter and son-in-law are away. I'm looking for a kitty cat mailbox."

She scanned the road ahead.

"I'm sure you'd be welcome to join us. I haven't seen the place, but from Reggie's description, it's one of a kind. There are high ceilings and lots of big old rooms. It's over a hundred years old. I'm looking forward to seeing her. It's been a while. She can be a bit of a sceptic, but that's Reggie for you. Her friend Donna, I can't remember her last name, is there too. Just think, Dan. You can be my mystery guest. I bet they'd like the company of a charming young man."

She slowed the vehicle as they came to a new-looking mailbox at the end of a winding drive. It looked professionally painted with a bunch of cats' faces on it.

"This is it," she crowed, hands at ten and two as she guided the old van down the tree lined drive. He smiled at her enthusiasm. She turned and lightly touched his arm, her face suddenly serious.

"Say, Dan. I should have asked. You're not allergic to cats, are you?"

CHAPTER EIGHT

Donna and I were upstairs, choosing which beds to make up for the night, when the dry sputter of a labouring engine accompanied the skid of stones outside.

Persia had arrived in her unmistakable orange gypsy wheels. She was not alone. A rangy young man in a tight T-shirt with dark blond hair to his shoulders slid out of the passenger seat and smiled admiringly at the house.

"I don't know who the cute guy is," I said, puzzled. "She didn't say she was bringing a friend. Let's find out who he is."

I backed away from the window, hurrying toward the stairs with Donna hot on my heels. The cats scattered in all directions. We tumbled out the door onto the porch just as Persia strolled around the back of the van. Graying braids swung past her slight shoulders as she cradled an old wicker hamper that had seen better years. Her face lit up in a broad grin.

"Reggie!" I kissed her soft cheek, then pulled gently away from the cloud of patchouli to introduce Donna.

"I believe you two have met. This is my friend Donna Cairns."

Persia beamed. "Oh, I think I remember you. We had a Tarot reading at my place, didn't we, some time ago?"

"No, but I did see you at a craft show in Thorold doing rock readings a few years ago."

Persia frowned in thought and bit her bottom lip trying to recall. She seemed to have forgotten her van passenger, now standing awkwardly a few paces behind her.

I beckoned to him. "Come join us!"

Sidling over with the self-consciousness of a stranger, he gave me a sheepish grin. Up close I could see he was taller than I thought, mid-twenties, on the skinny side. His T-shirt had a laid-back Bob Marley on the front of it, tucked into tight black Levi's.

Persia held multi-ringed fingers out to him like he was a child crossing the street.

"This is my new friend, Dan Riverton. Would you believe we just met down the road?" She squeezed his hand and continued brightly, effused with excitement. "Celestial forces have provided that we all meet here today. Can't you just feel the energy? Dan, meet my cousin, Reggie Bristow, and her friend, Donna... sorry, your last name?"

"It's Cairns. Nice to meet you both," she said, her eyes lingering on Dan.

Persia went on. "This amazing place is home to Reggie's daughter, Lisa, and her husband, Brad, who are away for the weekend. We'll be dining here."

Dan nodded politely to us, then bent to hoist the food hamper.

"Dinner has arrived!" Persia cried with a magician's flourish, then stopped dead.

"Oh wait." She clapped bejewelled fingers to her forehead.

Before we could say anything, she ran back to the van appearing seconds later waving a spray of dusty wildflowers.

She held them up to us like a trophy. "These beauties were waiting for our dinner table at the side of the road. I couldn't resist. Don't you just love daisies and sweet peas?"

I caught Donna's little smile as I put my hand out to hold the door. We took our time entering the house, checking around our feet.

"Just watch that the cats don't escape," I cautioned our new arrivals. "There are nine indoor cats living here and if any get out, I'm dead."

Dan hoisted his burden onto the kitchen counter with an audible gasp. Three disgruntled tabbies leaped away and scattered through the downstairs. The fourth and the biggest, old Sarge, I had finally figured out, remained on the counter and scrutinized us carefully, sniffing the hamper with his long nose.

Dan's was drawn to the menagerie. His head nodded as he tried to count how many cats roamed downstairs. He laughed and spoke for the first time to Sarge.

"Looks like you're part of a regular cat ranch, eh fella?"

His long fingers rubbed the big cat behind one ear, much to its pleasure. Donna wandered over to Winky, who sat wisely, his eye taking everything in from the staircase.

"This is amazing." Dan's eyes searched the main floor. "Old character homes are so cool. Persia said this one's over a hundred years old? New builds today wouldn't last that long. They practically go up overnight. All this interior brick and the rough-hewn beams would cost a fortune to duplicate."

I followed behind as they came to the living room. "Are you into construction, Dan? You sound so taken by this house."

"Not me." He gave a careless shrug. "I have a buddy in town, though, who's a finisher. He's always busy with new developments. Buyers want big houses with land, so country property is selling like hotcakes."

Persia walked around the kitchen, running her hands lightly over the walnut cabinetry.

"I grew up in an old place like this," she called from the kitchen pass-through. "My parents didn't have much money when they started out, so we moved in with my maternal grandmother who lived to be ninety! Remember playing in Grandma Hall's attic when we were kids Reggie?"

I considered the imposing Georgian manor Persia grew up in, though I hadn't thought about it when Lisa and Brad moved into this house.

"I sure do. And jumping on her overstuffed feather mattress. Our own trampoline. Gramma was such a sweet lady. We got away with just about anything at her house. That's why we liked sleepovers there so much."

We wandered back to the counter and sat on the stools. I made a motion with one hand to the vegan offerings. "Persia, do you mind if I store the dinner in the fridge, for now to keep it fresh? I think we have time for a drink, don't you?"

Pulling her attention from a sepia-toned photo of our grandparents on the wall, she nodded. We took care of removing the red linen-covered dishes from the oversized basket. It was quite a feast, judging by the number of bowls and platters. My spritely cousin was pumped, bouncing back and forth finding space for her goodies in the fridge. I almost hated to break the spell.

"There's wine, beer or soft drinks if anyone is interested." I took a quick count of the beers in the fridge.

Dan and Donna had returned to the living room, chatting by the picture window, taking in the fall panorama. They turned their attention to me.

"Red wine for me please," Donna answered.

Dan nodded in agreement. "Yeah, a glass of red wine would be good." I thought his smile looked somewhat odd. My warning flag unfurled fast.

"Okay, one bottle of red coming up!" I said, "Come and help me choose, cuz."

I took Persia's skinny arm gently until we were out of their line of sight, then pulled her roughly into the laundry room. Her eyes bugged out; her mouth opened wide in surprise.

"Reggie! What's wrong…" she sputtered, trying to pull herself from my clenched fingers. I closed the door quietly.

"Are you crazy?" I tersely whispered, then swung her around to face me.

"You've picked up a strange man on the road. We're miles from anywhere. What if he's a weirdo or something?"

I gripped her bony left arm tighter and fought an intense desire to shake her. She tossed back her long braids and gave a high giggle like a child.

"Oh, Reggie!" She gasped out of breath as if I were the crazy one. "Give me some credit, cuzzie. That lovely young man in there has been through great emotional trauma. His pain is palpable. I was privileged by the spirit to see his aura soon after we met. It was gray. That's conflict and sadness. But there were also green hues signifying loyalty and kindness. Really quite beautiful. His eyes are full of depth and understanding. He may have psychic abilities and not even know it." She gazed serenely at a plastic bottle of Tide. I dropped my arms and stared at her.

"Okay. He seems nice," I allowed. "But so did Ted Bundy. Where did he come from Persia? Where's his car?"

She smiled beatifically and spoke with a mellow, childlike voice. "Trust me. It will be revealed in time.

I didn't want to burden an already burdened soul with the third degree. If we are kind and tolerant, he will feel loved and accepted. Then we may learn how we can help him with his difficulties. I think he's kind of cute, don't you?"

I groaned at her innocence. "Just keep an eye on him, and not on his looks. I'll be watching."

I pulled out a bottle of merlot and a chardonnay from the wine cooler while she skipped off to join the others. When I emerged, a number of cats clustered on the pass-through to the kitchen counter. Apparently, they weren't perturbed by our young stranger either.

Donna and Dan sat on the overstuffed velour sofa, deep in discussion, two tabbies sprawled over their laps. Persia plopped herself next to Dan, crossed her arms, and gave me a saucy grin as I placed wine and glasses on the coffee table before them.

"Please help yourselves. If anyone is interested, Konzelmann makes a great merlot."

They started to open and pour the red. I made myself comfortable in a leather recliner opposite them. Somehow, I felt more relaxed, while still aware of the stranger's presence.

This was highly unexpected, my sense of responsibility entirely justified. As I observed them engaging in their happy chatter, I mentally configured an escape plan in case Dan wanted more than dinner. *Could three older women overtake him?* I figured Persia, the peacenik, would be useless in hand-to-hand combat. Donna was tall and well built, while I was short and husky. With provocation and a surge in our adrenalin, I figured we could do it if necessary.

I watched Dan's smooth hands and arms as he talked, his slim physique at ease. He sported those woven bracelets that young people favoured. He was good looking in a folksy kind of way, a John Cougar Mellencamp type. His reggae, peace-loving T-shirt made him seem harmless, but that wasn't it. As I watched him talk to Donna, I noticed the charm that women, particularly my generation, are often drawn to. His conversation was animated and he laughed easily. Donna glanced at me and winked her approval. She knew I was put out by my cousin's brazenness.

Persia held her crystal goblet high to catch the pale late afternoon light in a toast. "To a spellbound evening of magical occurrences that none of us may soon forget!" She flashed that same toothy grin of delight that had followed her from childhood.

Dan and Donna seemed pleased by Persia's ambitious toast and immediately picked up their drinks. I joined in and took an expectant sip. The merlot did not disappoint.

"I love this room." Dan gestured around with his glass. "The size! Man, my band could gig in this room. Way cool."

Donna sat forward, interested. "What instrument do you play?"

"Bass guitar. Our band is called Flatline.

Startled, we waited for an explanation.

"See?" he gestured. "We kill our audiences!"

A communal groan erupted.

"What kind of music?" Persia asked brightly, licking something from her thumb.

"Sort of a mix of rhythm and blues, rock, some jazz. I like retro myself. I grew up learning the words to folk songs from the '60s, thanks to my parents. They were big fans of Peter, Paul and Mary, and Gordon Lightfoot. I was the only kid in grade three who knew the words to 'The Wreck of The *Edmund Fitzgerald.*'" He flashed a brilliant smile at Persia. Her eyes cut away from him to the backyard vista of orange and vermilion foliage.

"That was such a sad song," she murmured to no one in particular. "It had a haunting melody that dispirited me. Maybe because it really happened. Those poor dead sailors, their families waiting to hear from them."

Abruptly she twisted back to us and smiled; her

mood visibly brighter.

"My favourite Lightfoot song is "Cotton Ginny." I always knew that if I gave birth to a little girl, I would name her that."

"Cotton Ginny?" I joked, unable to resist.

Persia responded with a look of distaste, poking her tongue out at me.

Donna held her drink with two hands on her lap, relaxing her head against the sofa cushion, taking no notice of our silly banter.

"You know, Dan"—she reflected with half-closed eyes—"my late husband, Jim, was in a rock band in the '60s called The Stray. They were quite popular on the local circuit. Reggie remembers those hot summer nights at The Cove in Long Beach."

"Who could forget?" I flashed a wistful grin. "You know it seems funny today, but the Cove was dry. Back then most of those who went were too young to drink. The legal drinking age was twenty-one, but it wasn't a big deal. We still had a great time. Just good entertainment, dancing our asses off, and hoping to meet someone dishy. The ones who wanted to drink went over the river, usually to Niagara Falls, New York, where they could get served at eighteen.

"Those were our salad days, right Reggie?" Donna recalled. "Getting all dolled up in the latest Carnaby look for Saturday night dancing. And you, the rocker girl, were hard to miss."

"Wait a minute." I laughed. "I wasn't the one called on stage at The Cove to shake my booty with the most popular, not to mention hottest, guy in high school!"

"My fifteen minutes of fame." She sighed.

"The Pony, wasn't it?" I added, then turned to the others. "Jim broke a number of hearts that night. It was obvious to his teenage fan club that Donna was the one. I bet you even remember what you were wearing and the song, right Donna?"

She giggled. "Of course, I do! A white lace Mary Quant mini dress, with white vinyl go-go boots."

Dan, eyes wide, gave a low catcall, while Persia sat fascinated.

"And what set it all off"—I interrupted with a sly glance at Donna—"was ultraviolet lighting, which made anything white, including teeth, light up like today's halogen lights. Miss Hot Stuff there shone like a beacon while making all the right moves."

"Of course, I did." Donna snickered into her hand.

Dan laughed. "So, Donna, what was the song they played for you?"

I gave her a wink, remembering their dance and how Jim hugged her at the finale.

"You will both know it." Her face beamed. "'You Really Got Me', by the Kinks."

Persia crowed, "I love that song!" She looked over at me. "I bet you were jealous, Reggie."

"Who wasn't? But there we had it. Our own rock-n-roll king and queen."

I watched Donna lounging back on the sofa, rubbing her wedding ring. She was lost in thought. It was the first time she discussed their budding romance since Jim's death.

"Man, I'd give anything to have grown up then." Dan stroked Spruce's neck with a gentle hand. "So many legends from that time. I've heard it said that the best music stopped after '72. Bob Dylan's one of my heroes."

Persia clapped her hands and squirmed with glee, her bloodstone pendant bouncing against her flat chest.

"I saw a show he performed in San Francisco way back when. It was a peace rally organized by anti-war protestors. And it *was* peaceful, thank God. Some weren't, you know. My friend Adrian's brother was over in Vietnam at the time. It really got to me, that anti-war sentiment. I was so glad to fly back home to Canada. Of course, I was only seventeen at the time. My mother didn't even know where I was, if you can believe it!"

Dan looked shocked. "Wait a minute. You just got up and left without telling anyone?"

Donna joined him. "Wow! My God, you were so young! Quite the free spirit eh?"

Persia hugged her chest at the memory and fell back on the sofa. She looked pleased with herself. "Oh, I did a lot of things my folks didn't know about. Highway hitchhiking, a bit of commune life, selling beaded jewellery I made to get money for pot. Very inventive. I was a Deadhead for a while, then fell for a psychic on the road who introduced me to the pleasures of sex and hallucinogenics." She sat up straight and gazed at me, pity masking her face.

"My poor cousin led the sheltered life, doing all the good-girl stuff. Sorority car washes, glee club, cheerleader, winter dance queen. As pure as virgin snow!" she teased.

"Oh stop. You rebelled to get your way about everything. Your parents were victims of your extreme manipulation. They wanted to be friends with you, not parents. Being an only child had its advantages. You even changed your name."

Dan hooted with laughter.

"Is there a guitar around?" Donna asked me. "Maybe Dan could play something. How about it?"

He got up from his chair and surveyed the room. "Sure, but I don't see one."

"Brad has a guitar." I squinted to remember if I had seen it here. To my knowledge, he hadn't played in years.

"Wait! Mine's in the van!" Persia ran to the front door, her pale muslin skirts flying.

"Watch the kitties!" I hollered after her.

Seconds later the screen door slammed and she returned cradling an old Gibson. She presented it to Dan who gave a low whistle as he took it from her hands.

"Very nice. Any requests, ladies?" he asked, tuning the strings. Snappy, the black and white cat, lolled at his feet.

Donna spoke up first. "Do you know 'Four Strong Winds'"?

Dan smiled at her. "Sure do. Ian and Sylvia. Great tune."

He started to strum, his slim, nimble fingers moving up and down the frets. Donna fell back, closed her eyes and breathed deeply.

"I love that song," she whispered.

The familiar melody wafted through the air as we watched Dan work his magic. I found myself humming along as he sang in a strong tenor. Persia joined in, and before everyone knew it, we were harmonizing to the old song. He enjoyed our enthusiasm, nodding and adding a few riffs. I was trying to think of my favourite oldie to request.

Persia piped up. "Outta sight, Dan. You're good. Do you sing lead in your group?"

He ran a hand through his blond fringe and shook his head.

"No. Dave Reddick's the singer. The rest of us do a bit of harmony, that's all."

He regarded me. "How about it Reggie? Which song made you fall in love?"

I put my head to the side, thinking. Joey, the hopper, was snoozing on his fleece bed, his gray and white head hanging comically over the edge.

"Hmmm, I'm not sure about falling in love because of a song, but let's see… Oh, I know. "Unchained Melody" by The Righteous Brothers. I was in grade nine. It was my first high school dance."

He played the song's opening chords and I was pleasantly surprised at the mellow tone. I had never heard it played in person by a guitarist. I watched his face, stern in concentration, as he strummed so effortlessly. Persia and Donna's obvious appreciation gave me a warm feeling inside, like going back to a simpler time, with family, being cared for and caring for others. When he finished the last chords there was silence.

Donna broke it gently. "I just love your voice. Do you write songs as well?"

He looked taken aback, then rubbed his bristled chin, and played a riff from the song 'Dueling Banjos.' Heaving a long breath, he cradled the six-string on his knee, one slim hand dangling over it.

"Yeah, I've tried some original stuff. I like writing songs. I can let a lot of stress out when I get into a song that just comes naturally. It's mostly for myself. I mean, I'm no Paul McCartney or John Lennon." He hummed, then stroked the strings softly, picking out bits of a light melody.

"Oh, don't be shy with us," Persia cajoled. "Let's hear something you wrote."

Donna and I followed suit. "Yes, play your favourite original." We sat forward, our hands clasped together like a couple of over-aged fangirls.

He blushed a bit. "Okay, but you asked for it. Hope there are no rotten tomatoes around."

The women grinned. His left hand cradled the guitar neck as quick fingers danced over the strings. The chords echoed with a soft muffled beat. He sang in a tender, clear voice.

I didn't know I could be so shaken.
The girls before always left my heart breakin'.
You were different, I sensed, from the moment we met.
A woman for sure, I would never forget.
I didn't know if you could love me the same way.
Then you came to me, and you showed me a new day.
Love has begun. It's much more than I've seen.
A life filled with you, now more than a dream.

Dan stopped playing abruptly and looked up from the guitar with a crooked smile. We urged him on for more.

"Sorry, ladies. That's all I've got so far for the lyrics." He pushed his hair back from his forehead. "I find the notes easier to place than the words. I need a chorus for that one. Hey, when it's ready, you ladies can back me up," he joked.

I was amused by the thought of us in a rock chorus. As a teen, I would've killed for the opportunity. Donna stretched out her arm to place her wine on the coffee table, then studied him. With a quick glance at me, she spoke.

"Dan, the passion you have for music is in your

incredible voice. It's a hard profession to break into, but isn't there some way you could make that dream happen? Lots of musicians have, when they searched long and hard, then finally made the right connections. I just watched a documentary on Quincy Jones. He propelled so many musicians to stardom. It was hard work for them, but the ones who made it had that special something that made them unique and desirable to the masses. Your talent is obvious. Maybe you just need to open yourself to the right connections."

"Yeah, I get that Donna," he said, rubbing his cheek thoughtfully. He coughed roughly into his hand. "It's been a dream of mine ever since I was a kid. My older brother, Chuck, taught me a few basic chords. Mom always said from then on, no one could get the guitar out of my hands." He grinned at the memory.

"Chuck left for college, then I took lessons when I was about twelve. It was so cool. My teacher at the conservatory told me I was a natural. The older I got, I'd dream of being onstage, like Clapton, girls screaming my name and tearing at their hair."

He dropped his hand from his whiskers and squared his shoulders. "You're right. It is tough to break into the biz. I can't make enough from local gigs to get a decent place to live and run my old beater of a car. We split the band's take and sometimes bookings are cancelled. That's why I live in my friend's basement. I've tried different jobs to fill the gaps, but I can't seem to stick with anything. It's like I have music on the brain or something. I'm too distracted and unhappy with anything else I've tried. I just want to practice my guitar. That probably sounds selfish, maybe even lazy. That's what Jess thinks anyway." His face fell and he returned to strumming.

"Who's Jess?" Persia piped up.

He looked up from the guitar.

"My girlfriend. Well… maybe not," he added. His lips formed a firm line and he shook his head. "She doesn't get it. We have fights 'cause she thinks I don't want to work. That's not it. I want to work doing this, playing great music and singing on stage. I want to entertain audiences who appreciate my singing and playing, like you guys." He looked at all of us, then singled out Persia.

"You saw me at the side of the road and brought me here. You took a chance on a stranger. But you saw something in me, or you wouldn't have helped me. You felt you could trust me and made me feel like a friend. Just like that." He snapped his fingers. "All you ladies have been awesome, especially for older people. Well, you know what I mean." his face coloured.

"Dan," I said, with a quick nod to my cousin. "I have to be honest. I was ready to strangle that woman over there for what I saw as a reckless move on her part."

Persia sat engrossed with a beaded bracelet on her wrist as I spoke.

"I guess she's a better judge of character than I am," I admitted. "We are often told to do what we love because life is so short. It's hard when the people closest to us don't understand. But I think it's important to be able to say that you tried. I too had a dream long ago."

—o0o—

CHAPTER NINE

I hesitated, not sure if I wanted to share this part of my personal history. I'd been just a kid, my ambition then seemed silly now.

His blond eyebrows shot up. "Yeah? Let me guess." He eyed me up and down, one hand cupped under his chin as if trying to get a read on me. Persia and Donna watched from the sofa.

"I'm gonna say you wanted to be a nurse and save lives," he concluded triumphantly; his hands raised high in a victory wave.

I nearly spilled my wine laughing at the thought of me, the selfless heroine, administering to the chronically ill and mortally wounded.

"Sorry, Dan. No Florence Nightingale here." I touched my nose. "My sniffer is too keen. That would definitely do me in." I lowered myself to the arm of the Bauhaus lounger and patted his shoulder.

Donna looked at the two of us, her blonde hair falling to one side.

"I honestly don't remember you telling me, Reggie. I can't even guess. Spill it, girlfriend."

"Okay, don't laugh. I was just a kid. I wanted to be a cowgirl and ride in the rodeo!"

Donna looked flabbergasted. "Really? I knew you loved horses. I mean we used to ride at the stables in Pelham, but who knew?"

Dan picked up the guitar and played a riff from "Home on The Range." I chuckled at his silliness and waved him away with one hand.

Regarding me blissfully, Persia said, "You would have made a wonderful Annie Oakley, Reggie. Like you, the woman was always independent. Why, she was able to ride her horse while standing on her saddle and taking a sure shot at a target. She was way ahead of her time." She clasped her fingers together, then went on in admiration.

"I can just see you putting those old cowpokes in their places, hands-on shapely hips, chin jutting out. Annie was a tough, sassy frontierswoman. Remember her singing to Buffalo Bill Cody?"

She lurched into a little-girl falsetto, strutting her skirts around the room. Like Annie, she dared that anything a man could do, she could do better.

All she needed was the cowgirl hat and fancy leather boots. I grinned at her boldness. Then Dan challenged her. He struck a loud chord offkey.

Persia jutted out her skinny hips, jumped in front of him and sang out that she certainly could.

Donna and I were enjoying their impromptu floorshow, egging her on to proclaim her superiority.

Persia came to a sudden stop, plopped her hands on her hips and cocked her head to one side as if to consider something. Then she popped her eyes wide, like a kid on Christmas morning.

"Annie Oakley had psychic abilities, if I remember correctly."

I threw back my head and coughed out a laugh.

"I must have missed that episode, Persia, but yeah, she was one tough cookie. Hey, enough about my childhood fantasies. What about yours?"

"Wait! Let me guess this one." Donna turned to Persia and, squinting, gave her the once over, while rubbing her chin.

Persia scrunched up her nose. "You'll never guess Donna. Reggie doesn't even know. It's my lifelong secret."

"Okay, I need some sustenance for this, folks." Donna took a hasty gulp of her merlot. "I want to say that you longed to be a gypsy and travel throughout Europe in a colourful caravan, but I have a feeling that isn't what you dreamt of. Hmmm, okay. How about a nun?" She giggled.

I slapped my good knee hard, then hooted, "A nun? Oh my God! Sister Sharon! Donna, you're a riot."

"Well, I don't know," Persia reasoned, appraising me. "I was quite devout as a child. I loved the rosary, all those shining beads! They were so pretty. It wasn't until I reached my teens that I began to question all beliefs. As a child, I was afraid of nuns. Those black habits were quite intimidating, you could never see their legs"

"Did you go to Catholic school?" Dan asked.

"Well yes, but not for long…" she looked quickly at me. I had my hand to my mouth, my shoulders shaking. "Reggie, I know you're bursting to tell, but I will, so don't."

I put the other hand over my mouth to hold back. Dan watched us as he scratched his head.

Persia leaped up knocking the coffee table in her haste. "I got caught smoking in the girls' washroom." She cackled gleefully, like a new age witch, her lean arms hugging skinny shoulders.

"I was twelve and Sister Carmelina caught me after some little brat snitched. So much for The Girls Academy of the Blessed Virgin. I was glad to leave the place. Too many rules and regulations. But you haven't guessed my dream, so I will tell you."

She paused dramatically, eyes sweeping her audience. "I wanted to marry John Maine, have five beautiful towheaded children, and live on a thriving farm filled with a Noah's Ark of animals and bountiful vegetable gardens." Her words tripped over each other in her excitement.

"Les Maine's little brother," I mused, thinking of a short, mouthy blond urchin in high school. "They lived in the Short Hills on a farm. Les was in my grade twelve class."

Donna spoke to Persia, who had picked up the ubiquitous Haylow from a neighbouring armchair and was rocking her like a baby.

"Well, no surprise there. I can see you tilling the land, wiping the sweat from your fevered brow as you pause to give birth, swaddle the infant, then continue working in the fields."

Dan snorted, then had the grace to redden, which made us all laugh. Unimpressed, Haylow leaped from Persia's arms. I got up and went back to the laundry room to fetch another bottle of wine while they chatted.

"It's my turn now," Donna called out. When I came back, she stood in the middle of the room, her arms gracefully positioned at her waist. I carefully moved to the three wine glasses trying not to spill as I crouched over the coffee table.

"Reggie?" She gave me a quizzical look. "Do you remember what I really wanted to do with my future? I did change my mind a couple of times, but this stayed with me."

"Oh, I think I remember, so I won't tell." I gave her a wink.

Persia jumped up, nearly knocking over her glass again. She caught it just in time and took an awkward swallow.

"Me! Let me guess. Wait…" She closed her eyes and held two long fingers to her forehead.

I pointed a stern finger at her and shook my head. "No visions allowed."

Dan lunged forward and pulled her hand from her shocked face. She uttered a high shriek, then slapped him away.

"Okay! Okay. But something was coming to me, I could feel it. Something pretty and pink with a lot of energy," she cried.

Donna twirled in a pirouette around the two, then performed a perfect plié. I grinned at her sense of fun as the others reacted to it. I did remember this dream of hers.

"A ballerina!" Persia shouted, clapping her hands.

"Yeah," Dan agreed. "You have great legs for that." He stopped, then stammered. "I, I mean, sorry, I meant…"

It was hilarious. Donna danced over to him on tiptoe and pulled him up to pirouette along with her. Our cat audience flew in all directions when Persia stood, lost her balance, and fell over the coffee table. We rushed over and offered help despite her protestations that she was fine. It didn't take much booze to make her giddy. I wondered if I should cut her off or let her loose. After all, she was an adult. Well, sort of.

Dan recovered from his embarrassment. "So, what happened to the little pink ballerina?"

"She fell out of a tree and broke her leg before she could become the next Veronica Tennant." Donna pouted.

"Aww, tough break. Whoops, here I go again," he joked. "So, you and Reggie go way back as friends? She said she knew what you wanted to be."

"Well, we weren't close in childhood. That came later, in grade nine." Donna moved over to sit beside me. "In fact, Reggie and I had a crush on the same senior. So, we didn't like each other in the beginning."

"Todd Ginsberg. 12B, very cute. My teenage dreams included sweaty nights of him groping me in the back seat of his Pontiac Bonneville."

Donna giggled. "Oh my, that's too funny. I could've had the same dreams."

"So, what happened?" Dan was curious now. Donna looked to me to take the conversational baton. "You tell. You're funnier." She elbowed me with a grin.

I snorted and rubbed my jaw. "He called me. My first boy phone call, mind you. And he seemed really interested... in both of us, as it turned out!"

Dan and Persia's jaws dropped.

"You mean he wanted both of you at the same time for sex?" she asked, her eyes popping.

We roared, hugging each other, weak with laughter.

"Oh, oh no!" I wiped my eyes. "Not that. Give us some credit. We didn't even know what a threesome was. We were good girls with wild imaginations, but we did keep our knees together."

Donna gave an indignant cry, pulling herself up straighter.

"He two-timed us!" she retorted. "He was leading us on, feeling quite the stud. After a few phone calls and the buzz on the girl grapevine, we figured it out and verbally attacked him in front of his buddies. He must have got a good ribbing about doing Romeo with two skinny grade niners. Reggie and I became good friends with a common enemy," she finished.

"I wonder what happened to him. He had incredible pale blue eyes, very sexy. The rumour was that he married a Victoria's Secret model from Toronto. That wouldn't surprise me."

"Why don't you look him up?" Dan suggested.

He pointed to Brad's roll top desk. Hermie, the sleepy gray kitty, lay sprawled in his day bed beside a Hewlett Packard laptop.

"We can Google him." I tossed my drink back.

The thought had never occurred to me, but after quaffing red wine for three hours, everything seemed possible. I hurried over to the desk, scaring the cat off with my rush, and turned the computer on. I was soon surrounded by three bearers of wine glasses.

"Do you know his full name?" Dan asked.

I turned to Donna. She was lost in thought. "Adam," she said. "I only remember because I would lovingly write our names together. I found them written all over one of my old yearbooks."

I typed in the name Todd Adam Ginsberg. There were a number of them from all over Canada. I narrowed the search with our former high school and town. Then I saw his pic. The eyes looked the same, but that was all.

"Oh, my God!" Donna clutched her glass and started a guttural laugh that spread to the rest of us.

Todd Adam Ginsberg, sixty-eight years of age, was the proud owner and director of Serene Passages, a funeral home in Toronto. He had not aged well.

"See what you guys gave up?" Dan chortled, shoulders shaking.

"I think he still has sexy eyes," Persia commented, lifting her glass for a slow sip.

I stared riveted. Todd had put on the pounds. Possibly one hundred. He looked so old!

"Well he looks kind," I conceded.

"Any other searches? Or shocks?" Dan leaned over for a better view. A wisp of musk met my nose.

Persia jumped up and down, her love beads clacking against her pendant. "Yes! Look up John Maine!" she squealed. "My one and only, John Amos Maine."

The screen soon filled with a multitude of John Maines. Persia's glasses glinted brightly in the light from the screen as she carefully studied the photos and bios. She shook her head slowly a few times. I was getting ready to suggest something else when she howled close to my ear.

"There! It's him. It's John."

We peered closely to the screen to see a pleasant-looking man in his sixties. He wore a clerical collar.

"Guess he didn't want all those kids," I said drily.

Dan and Donna laughed helplessly, while Persia studied the priest, two pale fingers pressed to her lips. She clutched my shoulder and exhaled loudly.

"Oh, I think I understand what has happened. You see, I was his one true long-lost love. We had an amazing connection that neither of us had ever experienced with anyone else. Our break up was all my fault. I got itchy feet and wanted to explore the world. He was a homebody. Look what happened. After we parted, he couldn't bear the thought of living without me so he eventually entered the seminary."

"Maybe he just found God," I suggested.

Persia shook her head, too intent on their tragic romance to get my humour. "No, I'm getting a sense of this, Reggie. The universe is telling me. It's his photo. It's showing me heartbreak and loneliness. Oh, and wait..." She moved her fingers to her furrowed forehead and paused dramatically.

"I see desperation! Oh, John I'm so sorry. I was young and foolish. We could have had such beautiful children!" she wailed, her face flushing a deep pink.

I raised eyebrows at Dan. It was hard not to laugh. His lips parted in a broad grin as he watched Persia's theatrics. I decided it was time to get away from John Amos Maine.

"Hey Dan, weren't you asking about palm readings earlier? How about it, Persia? Before dinner? Just the basics," I cautioned.

We shuffled over to the sofa. Persia gave an involuntary shiver, then plunked herself onto its wide arm, John Maine suddenly forgotten.

She blinked her eyes as if entering bright light, then held her hand out, palm up to Dan.

"Give me your predominant hand, the one you use the most," she explained. Dan wiped his right hand on his jeans, then held it out to her. She took it lightly and leaned forward to examine his palm, then squinted, and wrinkled her nose.

"Have you ever had your palm read?" she inquired.

"Nooo, this is definitely my maiden voyage."

Persia, her eyes owlish, examined us, then turned her attention back to the bewildered Dan.

"I can read your palm in ten minutes, then we will enjoy the best meal you've ever eaten!" she glowed with enthusiasm.

I was relieved by her change of direction. Maybe she wasn't getting drunk after all.

"Are you hungry, Donna?" I asked, turning to her.

She nodded. "Getting there. But I'd like to hear what Persia has to say."

Dan groaned as he pulled his hand away. "I dunno, ladies, if I'm into this hocus pocus stuff. Maybe I don't want to know what my future will be."

Persia grabbed his hand back abruptly. "Look." She stroked her finger down the wide centre of his smooth palm. Her trim nails featured the natural look, no nail polish.

Donna moved her head closer for a better view.

Persia was engrossed.

"That's your lifeline there, Dan." She showed him. "See how it crosses your palm? There are only two little breaks in it. See them? They may indicate health concerns or other disturbances over the course of your life. Look, you have a long lifeline. According to what I see here, you will be on this earth for many years to come. You must have good genes."

"Or dry skin," I observed. She made a face at me and the other two laughed.

"What about his love life?" Donna asked with a cheeky grin. She moved gracefully around to Dan's other side and watched.

"Let's see." Persia concentrated. "Your palm is quite smooth – after all you are young – so cup it a little, like this."

She curled his fingers inward which deepened the lines.

"Oh, Danny boy, you are going to be in love a few times. See this area here?" Their gray and blond heads bent together.

I looked at Donna and she gave a thumbs up.

"Yeah, I see that. What does it mean?" he asked. He sounded concerned. Maybe Persia had a convert after all.

She gave his hand a gentle squeeze. "You will marry, but later in life. In the meantime, though, I would say you will have an interesting love life!"

"No surprise there." I stood to direct the others. "Come on. The feast awaits. Let's set the dining room table while Persia arranges her cuisine."

Donna started toward the kitchen and I followed, humming a little tune that had popped into my head. Dan, now on his knees, played with Winky, pulling a deranged looking catnip mouse along the area rug.

"I hope everyone's hungry." Persia gestured at the milk-white crockery laid out on the counter.

"There's our appetizer of vegan feta cheese, generously sprinkled over grilled organic beets, spinach, arugula and green beans."

She swept a graceful hand to a large platter of what looked to be small triangles of pastry.

"This is grilled tempeh which is fermented soybean. It has a unique, nutty taste. I like to top it with a honey ginger sauce to bring out the distinctive flavour," she explained, pleased at our approving looks.

"I have included vegan naan, which I freshly baked this morning. It is wonderful for soaking up the tasty sauces."

Dan appeared at the other side of the kitchen island. "Hey, this looks really good." We eagerly agreed. It did look good. Maybe I was too quick to judge vegan delights.

Persia held up a smoked glass dish filled with a creamy concoction. "And this, my friends"—she gazed lovingly at the proffered bowl—"is my piece de resistance. You'll really love this Reggie, with your sweet tooth. I have named our dessert Coconut Sweet Dreams. It has a strawberry sorbet base, which is covered with fresh field berries, pear slices and glazed pineapple, topped with vegan lemon curd, maple syrup, then garnished with coconut and mint."

Donna shook her head at the array of food. "This is tantalizing, Persia. Let's eat!" She laughed.

We found our cutlery and plates, then dug in. I was famished, as I'm sure the others were. No holding back from the guests. We piled our plates high and moved into the dining room, choosing chairs around the round oak table.

Persia held up two hands like she was about to stop traffic.

We looked up expectantly.

"I just had a thought."

I quickly wondered if we would be asked to thank the universe.

"Is anyone allergic to sunflower seeds?"

—o0o—

CHAPTER TEN

Lisa checked her phone for the fifth time, then held it up for Brad to see the screen. They were about to enter the Brighton Room where the annual Pause for Claws dinner and presentations would take place. Throngs of cat devotees sauntered their way around the white linen covered tables, checking seating arrangements and schmoozing in a low buzz.

"I've sent five messages and called three times in the last hour. No answer. Why isn't Mom checking her phone?" She tugged on a loose lock of her hair.

"Come here, hon. I believe we're under the Bs for Bristow." His hands fell on her shoulders as he gently steered her over to their designated table. Once she was comfortably seated, he cradled her hand, massaging it with tender fingers.

"We have a big house now," he said quietly. "Your Mom must be out of hearing range. Maybe she's showing Donna around outside. Aren't they nature lovers? You didn't expect that she'd have her phone on her at all times, did you?"

"Of course! But I haven't been able to get an update for two hours. I want to know if the kitties ate all their food. We never stay away overnight. They may be upset that we haven't returned and lose their appetites. You know how Nukkers gorges when she's especially nervous and then throws up." She dropped her head against his chest. He took her small hands again in his large ones and examined her face. She was lovely in her silver-gray sheath, the tiny, satin rosettes on one shoulder, lustrous curls falling over the other. He loved her, even if that meant feeling more like an older brother than a husband occasionally. Like now.

"I think Reggie will be fine, honey. Geez, there are two moms at the house. They're probably rocking to the oldies and playing with the kitties. Put women with wine and song and you're talkin' a good time. Did you notice how taken they were with our place? I think they'll be settled in by now, having a drink, getting ready to have dinner. Look, get your presentation out of the way, then try texting again. You can tell her you were a rock star up there. There's a wonderful crowd of philanthropists here tonight just waiting to hear from you." He gave her a wink.

She studied his broad, handsome face and started to reply when their friend, and Lisa's mentor, Muriel Peabody appeared out of nowhere. The older woman was resplendent in a shimmering blue chiffon cocktail dress, her silver spun hair swept up in a jewelled French twist. Diamond and pearl clusters twinkled from her large ears. As director of Pause for Claws, she was the go-to person for every detail of the annual fundraising dinner. She thrived on her position in the organization and it showed.

"Darlings!" she gushed; her face wreathed in a smile. She gave Lisa's arm an affectionate squeeze, while a torrent of glittering bangles cascaded down to her liver-spotted hand.

"We are so looking forward to your presentation. Members have asked about the latest designs for backyard protection. The video you sent to me was excellent. I hooted at your kitties' antics in what can only be described as a feline wonderland. Your cats are bursting with health and vitality. A far cry from their beginnings. You provide so well for them."

She smiled conspiratorially and stooped toward them, in a cloud of Chanel No.5. "And, for our organization of course. We can't thank you enough!"

She straightened herself, patting her coif, bright blue eyes surveying the grand dining room. Paige

Marcus interiors had done a marvellous job with the royal blue and gold motif. The stage display was particularly effective. A variety of vibrant plush cats adorned the bunting, giving it a whimsical look. Pungent aromas of succulent prime rib and freshly baked ciabatta filled the air.

Lisa timidly touched her fingers to the director's hand, which rested on the back of her chair.

"We are thrilled to be part of such a fine organization." She blushed, her nerves buzzing. Muriel smiled regally at her, nodding.

Emboldened. Lisa pressed on. "I think I mentioned to you in an email that the video I'm presenting after dinner was made at our previous home. The fencing is shown there but in a much smaller perimeter. Of course, it makes it easier to see them all playing. We bought little trampolines and pup tents which will amuse our friends tonight, I'm sure. They have so much fun bouncing and hiding from each other. I could watch them for hours. Three weeks ago, we moved to a much larger house outside Dunnville. It's a perfect home for our crew. I can't wait for you to visit. Once the fencing is set up there, I hope soon, our babies will have a half-acre of freedom outdoors. I really love the peace and solitude of country living. They will too. Above all, they will be safe. That's my main concern."

Muriel's head bobbed up and down. "It sounds like a paradise for you all. How splendid." Her attention was suddenly diverted by a young woman in an orange crepe floor-length dress, sporting black velvet cat ears. As the woman swung her ample hips around the guests' tables, turning a number of male heads, Lisa watched her slink away through the crowd of happy onlookers.

"Excuse me dears." Muriel moved away from them in the young woman's direction.

"Oh, Darcy! Yoo-hoo! I need something," she called out, waving a manicured hand. Muriel vanished into the throng.

Their table was filling up. Marsha, the social convenor, slid into the chair next to Lisa's. She was a short, dark woman of blended ancestry, who looked quite festive in a bright green mini dress. Too mini, Lisa thought with a quick look at the woman's heavy legs. She checked her own hemline. It was fine.

"Hey! Thought I might see you guys at the opening last night," she said, tossing her pearl evening bag onto the table.

Brad turned to Marsha with a laugh. "It's hard enough to pull Lisa away for one night."

Lisa nodded frowning. "We just moved to the

country, Marsha. Everything happened at once. There's so much to do. I feel torn in too many directions. I like your dress," she added with a smile.

Marsha pursed her full lips and looked at her.

"Thanks. Yes, moving is stressful. I've done my share of it. Especially after my divorce. Isn't that girl you said you were training taking care of your cats?"

Lisa dropped her gaze to her lap.

"No, Grace is sick," she muttered. "I would have cancelled coming tonight, but I didn't want to let you all down." She gave Marsha an anxious glance, then confided, "My mother and her friend are taking care of our cats. I'm a bit worried. Mom's never watched them before and she doesn't know the house. I've tried to get her on the phone but…"

Brad interrupted. "I keep telling her it'll be fine." He wrapped a playful hand around Lisa's neck, then stood to hail a friend at a table nearby.

Marsha began to laugh, then regarded Lisa, her hazel eyes amused.

"She raised you. How hard could a bunch of cats be for one night? She has a friend to help. Your mom would phone you guys if there was an emergency." She lowered her voice. "Listen, I don't know if you heard the latest about Muriel?" Marsha slid her chair closer, to confide. Lisa jerked her head back, almost hitting her.

"Muriel? What about Muriel? We were just talking to her."

Marsha rushed on, fuelled by the thrill of gossip. "Rumour has it that Selma Daniels is after Muriel's position. The Board has discussed replacing the grand dame off and on for some time. It's funny you haven't heard anything."

Lisa bit her bottom lip then glared at Marsha. "Muriel is wonderful. She does everything. She knows so many contributors who love her. She's been our director forever!"

Marsha's face lowered uncomfortably close again, her breath thankfully peppermint.

"That's just it, Lisa," she whispered tersely like she was about to reveal a dirty secret. "It's time for new blood, fresh ideas for expanding our donor base... new promotional venues. Selma has incredible clout in higher circles and her tech marketing skills are second to none. She works for Blake Barnsdale, one of the biggest law firms in Toronto. And she's been consulted by our group regarding business proposals. It goes without saying that she's a cat lover and has been extremely generous in that regard. Let's face it, Muriel has done what she can, and done it all right up to now, but she is getting on. I mean she's pushing seventy-five. Time for her to move over." She stopped to lean back and take a sip from her water goblet.

Lisa propped her chin on her hand and shook her head glumly while scanning the now seated guests.

"Poor Muriel," she pouted, winding a stray lock of hair around her finger. Suddenly angered, she turned on the convenor.

"This will kill her, Marsha. Pause for Claws is her life. I mean, Selma is fine I guess, but I don't like her as much as Muriel. She doesn't have that warm, nurturing personality. Muriel is like everyone's mother or grandmother. I've known her for six years, longer than you have, she always makes me feel like the most important person she's ever talked to. She takes a special interest in people. I don't think Selma is like that. Muriel has the personality for her position. Why, she's planning to come all the way to Dunnville to visit our cat crew and see our new home! I've sent kitty pics and she's so excited. She even remembers all their names. My own mother can't remember them all. I wish you hadn't told me," she blurted, arms crossed, flouncing back in her chair.

"Oh, Lisa! Come on. It's not the end of the world." Marsha laughed. "Haven't you heard of attrition? Granted, there isn't any mandatory retirement age anymore, but it's just good business practice, whether in a volunteer organization or not. If people don't keep up with the times, they outlive their usefulness in the job market. Muriel will find new venues for her nurturing. Maybe baby cuddling at the hospital." She gave Lisa's shoulder a light squeeze.

She shrugged away from Marsha's hand. "It's not fair. I know Brad will be as angry as I am. Maybe I won't tell him."

She turned away to watch her husband socializing with a jovial group at the next table. Marsha followed her gaze.

"He probably knows and didn't want to upset you, that's all. Listen, Muriel is no dummy. I bet she knows which way the wind is blowing."

Marsha studied her for a moment, searching her face.

"I didn't mean to upset you. I know you're a fan of Muriel's. I thought you knew and we could dish a bit about it, that's all. Things change, that's life, and change can be good. It comes down to a vote. Majority wins."

She reached for her evening bag and rooted through its contents retrieving her phone to make a call.

Lisa turned quickly away from Marsha searching

once more for Brad. He'd disappeared. A sudden intense dislike for Marsha made Lisa wish the woman was sitting at another table, or better yet, not at the conference at all. Where was Brad? Why had he kept this terrible news from her?

Muriel was their dear friend, like family. They met at the Toronto cat fanciers show years back when Lisa met Brad. Muriel was thrilled that Lisa had discovered such a fine man, though she hadn't met him herself.

They had maintained a correspondence over the years. Muriel was a woman Lisa looked up to. A role model. Her thoughts fought with each other as she kept eyeing the room. If Brad knew and didn't tell her, perhaps he had withheld other awful news from her. A flush rose up her neck, a sure sign of distress. Maybe her blood pressure was elevating. She scooped her curly hair up in one hand and took a sip of sparkling water.

"Show's about to begin, ladies," Brad's pleasant voice came from behind her. His soft fingers caressed her shoulder as he took a seat.

She would wait until after her presentation to say anything to him. This was not the time for a scene, especially with gossipy Marsha there as a spectator. *Poor Muriel.* Lisa watched the well-loved director stride purposefully to the podium and happily take in the dining-room assemblage. The hubbub died down as she pulled the microphone towards her.

"Good evening my friends, and friends to be," she welcomed, with a wide smile.

"Our annual Pause for Claws Conference gives us an opportunity to connect face to face with our membership and hopefully new members. We have a lovely evening planned for you all. Rex Donelli has graciously accepted our invitation to play musical selections at the baby grand. I may confide in you now, with his permission of course, that he is engaged to be married next month. I think you will find his talented repertoire appropriate to our delightful evening."

She winked and held out a graceful hand to a middle-aged man in black coat tails seated at the piano. He stood, grinned unabashedly and bowed with gusto to the applauding guests. Muriel adjusted her glasses, checked her papers on the lectern and resumed her introductions.

"After dinner, while we are enjoying our scrumptious dessert, Carman Hicks, director of the Toronto Humane Society, will be speaking on behalf of their fine organization. We are honoured to have him with us this evening. As I'm sure you all know, Mr. Hicks has a special relationship with our organization. Pause for Claws was the original pet charity for the Toronto Humane Society back in 1995. This was during his administration and largely due to his interest in promoting the first official rescue group for cats in the GTA.

"Since that time, we have worked tirefully…" She stopped, seeming to lose her place, then apologized and resumed with a reddened face. "I'm sorry, *tirelessly* to secure services in our community to develop affordable spaying and neutering clinics. This liaison has increased public awareness of issues pertinent to animals, cats in particular.

"Following Mr. Hick's address will be Ms. Dolores Marsico, fundraising convenor of Pause for Claws. Ms. Marsico will give a summary of this year's donation drives and new projections for next year."

She paused, adjusted her bifocals and scanned the audience. Her face reddened again and she looked confused.

"Oh dear, please bear with me. I think I'm having what they call a senior moment!" She laughed nervously, searching her papers.

"Of course, how silly of me," she nodded, then affirmed in a loud voice, "Lisa is up after Dolores."

Marsha arched back in her chair to look at Lisa

and raised an eyebrow. Lisa scowled at her.

"We round out our evening with a commentary and video presentation by Ms. Lisa Bristow. Lisa and her husband Brad Quinn have been members of our group for many years and are the proud owners of nine rescues who continue to thrive.

"So many people make our organization a community success. I feel privileged to work with you all. I want to take this opportunity to extend a very big thank you to the generous donors who make Pause for Claws an important part of our community. We truly couldn't do it without your support!

"So now, without further ado, ladies and gentlemen, a delicious dinner will be served. Enjoy a wonderful evening and bon appetite." She gathered her papers and hurried off the stage. The crowd resumed a hum of chatter.

Lisa turned to Brad, her face grave.

"Something's wrong with Muriel," she whispered to him. "She wasn't herself up there. I hope she's okay."

Brad nodded as he watched the director move between the busy tables.

"It wasn't like her usual presentation. Maybe she has the jitters tonight. It's only once a year, and she is getting up there," he said.

Thinking Marsha was ripe for a comment, Lisa turned her back to the woman and spoke to Brad.

"I think I'll feel better once I get some food into my stomach. It smells so good." She rubbed her tummy.

He was quick to offer a brimming bowl of crusty golden rolls. "Dig in, honey. Lots more to come!"

The sweet strains of Andrew Lloyd Webber's "Memory" drifted through the air.

—o0o—

CHAPTER ELEVEN

"I don't know about the rest of you, but I ate too much!" I patted my distended belly and slid my chair back with a groan. Despite my earlier reservations, I relished every vegan dish, especially the dreamy coconut dessert. My Keto diet would wait.

"I never knew vegan food could be so tasty." I lifted my full wine glass to the glow of the black iron chandelier.

"To our superb chef of the evening, Persia Orly!"

We all clinked glasses, then Dan stood and held his hand out to all of us. "And to the best dinner dates a guy could ever hope for."

We hooted at his bon vivant, then I held my merlot to him for another toast.

"And to the minstrel with the most!" I added.

The crimson vintage glittered high over the remains of our feast on the old oak table. Persia took a timid sip of her drink, her thin lips hovering over the rim.

"This is so remarkable," she cried, wiggling her shoulders and waving her bright bracelets in an arc around the room. "This historic house, brimming with magical energy, the positive vibes that encircle us, nine extraordinary cats, whose lives have been saved, a magnificent evening with my favourite cousin and two incredible new friends who have entered my celestial orbit." She finished, blushing and out of breath.

"Same goes here cuz, but I may have to cut you off. Your face is on fire!"

Her laugh tinkled high, multi-ringed fingers flying to her cheeks.

"Oh, I do blush with red wine, Reggie, but I'm also quite invigorated tonight. I sense a convergence of some kind. It feels like a journey and we are the travellers about to arrive at our destination. The energy in this room is crackling. Can't you just feel its charge? Look, even the cats sense it."

She moved her chair back, to present Winky, who regarded us solemnly from his cushy upholstered perch. He didn't look prepared for any oncoming adventure. His golden eye almost seemed ready to droop.

Dan regarded the cat for a minute, then slid back in his seat, one arm thrown casually along the back of Persia's chair.

He studied her for a moment. "I was just wondering something. Like, who does your palm readings and all that other spiritual stuff?"

She crossed her hands on the table, observed them lovingly, then spoke.

"I have an eighty-six-year-old gentleman friend in New York City, Cosmo Obsidian. He is an amazing spiritualist. His specialty is channelling, which is basically getting in touch with departed spirits. It's fascinating to watch. He asks you to write your name on a piece of paper, then he takes another pencil and makes circles over your name. At some point, he receives messages from the deceased which he passes along to you.

"I wish I could visit him more often, but he is a very busy man. Even at his age, he still drives to many psychic fairs, if you can imagine. Of course, he has to be aware of his energy limitations and not tax himself. You would love him. He's a dear little man, just over five feet tall with a port-wine stain that covers half of his face. I found it a bit distracting when I first met him, but he put me right at ease. He has a sweet, mysterious nature that draws one in. And he's quite flirtatious with both sexes, much to their delight!

"I've known him for twenty years. He's rarely steered me in the wrong direction. Once in a while, he'll call out of the blue to advise me just when I need it most. He's so gifted in his accuracy. I will happily listen to him, even if it means giving up something I truly want.

"For instance, the last time he called me, I was considering buying a small house not far from my apartment. My father is always telling me to invest in property instead of paying rent. I even had Papa go through the place with me after I was charmed by my first visit. It was a cozy little two-bedroom cottage with gingerbread trim and needed work like painting and decorating, but I love to do that. I told the agent I would think about it. Papa said it would make a good starter home, and I was about to draft an offer with the agent when my little friend, I nicknamed him Obie, short for Obsidian of course, phoned me.

"He had had a vision of a burning house with money pouring out through the windows! The amulet he gave me seven years ago was lying on the sidewalk in front of the burning house, so he knew that it was a sign to contact me. Needless to say, I changed my mind about buying the place. I told the realtor I wasn't ready to buy yet. Three months later after it sold, I noticed a truck for wet basements in the driveway." She fell back on her chair with a gasp and said, "That might have been my fate. Dear Obie!"

We laughed at her theatrics, then Donna asked, "I saw you reading Tarot cards, as I mentioned before, are there other things you consult?"

Persia rubbed her hands slowly together and warmed again to the topic.

"Well, I do make other consultations – crystals, astrology charts, runes—"

"Ruins? What are those?" Donna asked, raising her eyebrows.

Persia chuckled, then corrected her. "Runes, like June with an 'r'. They're beautifully polished stones with ancient symbols painted or etched into them. They provide guidance. For me, I prefer Tarot or palmistry, but that's just my preference. Obie uses all modalities for journeys to the unknown and unseen. One consistent thing he has foretold me over the years is that my life partner will be a man in uniform. I was shocked the first time he told me that, thinking of a military man, which is not on any radar for me!" She grimaced.

"Well, a uniform doesn't necessarily mean a soldier," I said. "How about the hot night manager at your local McDonalds?"

Donna and Dan guffawed loudly as his knee hit the underside of the table.

Persia squealed. "Reggie! You are incorrigible."

I went to slip my arm around her for a hug. She made a mock protest, then fell back into her chair aghast.

"Eww! Me with a beefy meat-eater? I would rather die." she sputtered, then halted her carnivore critique suddenly, as if something had occurred to her.

"Speaking of death," she said, her luminous eyes studying the room, a lone finger tapping her chin. Our laughter was gone, replaced by puzzled looks.

"Nothing of ill intent," she hurried on, "but I'm getting something here. Something about past lives. Spirits of the dearly departed. Old, remote houses have been known to shelter restless souls searching for their former families. Just think back in history how often the sick died in their beds, regularly in the darkness of night."

My neck hairs stood at full attention while I waited to see where this was going.

Persia craned her neck slowly up as if to locate said, dead people. We followed her gaze. Fortunately, there were no apparitions.

"Six cats," she said, nodding to herself, seemingly satisfied with her observation.

We looked at one another. Dan scratched the back of his head and frowned. *Maybe coffee, copious amounts for her.*

Persia's small glasses caught the light of the chandelier over our heads.

I checked the room myself and counted, Winky, Snappy, Montana, Spruce, Joey and Sarge, watching from various vantage points in the shadows. The others, Haylow, Hermie and little Nukkers had apparently decided to forgo the evening's festivities. The eerie glow of the surrounding cats' steady gaze unnerved me and I was about to suggest moving to the living room.

"Okay, Persia, there are six cats here. Why don't we go and get—" Distracted by whatever she was sensing, she cut me off.

"Just a minute Reggie…it's a sign. There's something to be done," she explained patiently. "It may indicate a coming epiphany through a ceremony of some kind, but this is a bit different." She stopped speaking and closed her eyes. We waited, watching.

After a few seconds, a low hum buzzed from her throat. Her eyes blinked open, as if she had just awakened. "How do you feel about me conducting a seance? It's been a long time since I arranged one, but I'm really getting something from this house, and this room in particular. What do you think?"

My mind reeled. This was unexpected. I felt rather uncomfortable at the thought of engaging in an activity I knew so little about. Sure, it might be fun for a few laughs, but Persia tended to be all business with her beliefs. She would take it seriously, and I really wasn't certain what she was capable of. Departed souls, spirits? My instincts said no.

I glanced at Donna, whom I thought of as most recently bereaved. She appeared calm and very into Persia's proposal.

Dan called out, "More hocus pocus!" and wiggled his fingers at us all.

I smiled at his sense of fun, but I still had concerns.

"Well, I don't want to be a wet blanket," I said slowly, weighing my words. "But I don't know about this. I would hope you're not going to release wandering spirits here. Lisa would not be amused if weird stuff started happening in her new home."

She nodded. "I absolutely respect your concerns, but I must say I feel very positive energy here right now. Should that change at any time during the seance, I will excuse us from participation. Does that help?"

"What about you guys? Round out our evening with the spirit world or not?"

Dan held up his right hand to us all like he was about to receive an offering.

"Hey look, I had my first palm reading and I feel great. I say go for it."

Donna agreed with him. "Why not, Reggie? Like Persia said, bad vibes and we're out."

Not wanting to be the stuffy worrywart anymore, I chimed in, "Why not indeed. What do we do first, cuzzie?"

"First, we clear the table." Persia motioned to the detritus of our dinner strewn about the napkins and tablecloth.

"Shall we do the dishes now?" Donna asked as we started to gather our plates and cutlery.

I shook my head. "Oh, let's not. We can just move everything to the counter and I'll fill the dishwasher later."

Persia stood, hands on her narrow hips, sharp eyes appraising the dining room once more.

"Perfect. I have candles and the Ouija board in the van. I'll set it up right on the table. And we have four people. Even numbers work best. I'll be right back!" She disappeared into the hallway while we prepared the room. It seemed unusual to me that some cats had jumped from their climbers and were approaching me, rubbing against my legs. A couple of tabs, Spruce and Haylow, crouched low, then jumped up on the table and stretched themselves, arching and writhing in pleasure.

Dan saw them from the kitchen and laughed. "Well look at that. They're getting ready for a seance, too. I heard cats can sense spirits."

"I've heard that too," I said. "My mother, who was very superstitious, told me many years ago that cats can see souls rise at the moment of death. She claimed that they actually arched their necks back and would let out a blood-curdling cry."

Donna shivered as she reached over to get the last dessert plate. "That's just creepy. I know I don't want to see that."

I patted her shoulder, then picked up a stack of scraped plates to put them into the sink. We wrapped up our cleaning by wiping down the table as Dan moved our wine glasses to make room.

Persia came through the front door balancing the evening's entertainment. Her steady hands carefully removed four creamy tapers from an old Dutch Masters cigar box. Underneath was a child-sized handkerchief embroidered with tiny yellow ducks that held a tarnished candle ring. After setting up the candles and lighting them with matches from the cigar box, she turned to me, all business.

"Let's see." She tilted her head to look around the square table. "Reggie, you sit there. Donna on this chair. Dan here. We sat, expectantly, as she moved quietly about the room, a hint of patchouli in her wake. She looked at the staircase behind her, then turned to the living room.

"Where's the light switch for this room, Reggie?"

I was about to show her, when she found it at the back of the sideboard. She switched it off in one quick motion. The room was immediately bathed in darkness, save for the glow of a small night light in the kitchen and the four lit candles on the table.

Slowly she lowered herself onto her chair with a deep breath, adjusting her glasses. Their reflection by the candlelight enlarged her eyes, giving her a strange, much older appearance. I was now aware of how still the room had become. Donna and Dan's faces looked hollow as their eyes trained on her slow measured movements by the flickering flames. Persia cleared her throat abruptly, her voice dropping to a purring, soft tone.

"Before we begin"—she instructed, placing the Ouija board with reverent hands on the middle of the table—"it is necessary to know if anyone here has difficulty acknowledging the spirit world, or is afraid to do so." Her gaze regarded each of us in turn.

"I think I can do this," I spoke as quietly as Persia had. "It is a bit spooky, though, I must admit."

Dan turned his body to me and touched my arm,

"Don't worry, my damsel fair. I will protect you from all evil spirits."

I gave an uneasy laugh then looked across the table at Donna. It reassured me that she seemed charged for this new experience. Her soft features lit up in anticipation.

"I find this very interesting," she said. "I love to try unusual things and I feel comfortable with all of you in this beautiful place. I have faith in you, Persia. If something scary happens, can't we just turn on the lights?"

"Of course, we can." She rested a gentle hand on Donna's shoulder. After a deep breath herself, Persia began.

"We will start by closing our eyes, which will enable the relaxation process. Now we continue this process with simple breathing, my friends. Deep, slow breaths," she guided in a slow, dreamy monotone. "Breathe in... then breathe out. In... then out, relaxing all muscles and opening the portals to your minds. There is nothing to fear. We are all friends... Breathe in, then out.

"Now, take hands around the table, then close your eyes once more and let your mind drift upon waves of serenity. Breathe softly in time to the motion of the waves... in then out. This peaceful relaxation welcomes the spirits to come, to engage in communication, gently, gradually at their discretion.

"Allow your mind to drift in the darkness, still taking a deep breath in… and as you release it, relax your neck, shoulders and arms. Take another deep breath… release, then feel the tension drift away from your legs and from your feet. Continue to deeply breathe in… then slowly out, expelling all fears, worries, and tensions. As we embrace our peace, we create a welcoming place of love and trust. Breathe deeply in… and out…"

After a peaceful minute, I peeked at the threesome through squinting eyes. They were definitely drifting. Donna's slim shoulders drooped and her blonde head hung forward, while Dan, his mouth slack, looked upon the verge of snoring. Persia held their hands as if in silent prayer. My hands had gone icy and I quickly wondered if Dan or Donna could feel it in my fingers. I was edgy. Maybe it was my overeating at dinner or residual concern about this whole ritual.

Then it hit me. I'd forgotten to check my phone for hours. With all the unexpected distractions this afternoon, I just didn't think of it. There would be urgent messages from Lisa, I was certain. Well, another half-hour wouldn't hurt, I reasoned, chicken that I was. I didn't want to interrupt things here or the spirits might get angry.

I smiled to myself. I'd text her right after the seance, which I hoped would be short and sweet. Of course, I wouldn't mention the seance, or Persia, or Dan. They would be gone by the time Lisa and Brad returned home tomorrow. My attention returned again to the group.

Persia continued her spell, softly calling us back to open our eyes to the Ouija board and prepare for a possible visit from the spirit world. I blinked, then watched as she picked up an old heart-shaped piece of wood and lovingly caressed it with a silver-ringed thumb.

"This is called a planchette." She held the wooden triangle reverently in both hands. Her soft blue eyes moved from Dan to Donna, then back to me.

"Who shall we summon this evening?" she asked.

My dear mother came to mind. She passed away ten years earlier. I was almost sure her advice would be the same after death as in life: "Regina, why in the love of God can't you find a decent man?" My thoughts were sidelined by Donna's voice.

"My husband, Jim. I'd like to hear from him."

My surprise must have shown.

"It's all right, Reggie, I want to try this."

I couldn't help feeling worried. This hocus pocus,

as Dan called it, was uncharted territory for all of us, except my cousin. But I recognized the determined set of my friend's mouth and knew there was no going back. I gave her a quick thumbs up.

Persia tucked a stray hair back into a braid, nodded at the board and asked us to put two fingers each on the planchette. Being the shortest, I had to stretch across the wide oak table to manage it. I wanted to laugh at how strange our fingers looked crowded together and wondered if I was getting tipsy or falling under some spell. The flames from the ivory tapers made dark wavy designs along the extremities of the room. Glowing cats' eyes gazed spellbound from the darkened windows along the old brick walls. They were now back on their climbers. I counted six again, the same six. My neck hairs stood on end.

"We humbly invite, kind spirits," Persia intoned, her face solemn and ethereal, "our dearly departed brother, Jim Cairns, to join us this evening. His loving wife, Donna, requests his presence."

My awkward fingers gently touched the planchette. Four serious faces watched it without wavering, for any sign of movement. Just when my right arm was beginning to numb, the planchette moved.

Mesmerized eyes followed its slow progress to L,

haltingly to O, then V, then E. There was an abrupt stop. After a long pause, it resumed its cautious journey via our outstretched fingers to Y, O, U in purposeful succession. *Love you.* Dan drew in a sharp intake of breath and stared at Donna with disbelieving eyes. She glanced up from the Ouija board at me, her eyes brimming with unshed tears. Persia turned to her.

"How are you feeling?"

Donna rubbed under her eyes with shaking fingertips. My heart pounded a hard tattoo in my chest. The shadowed room shrank, four brick walls closing in on us, the cool air musty. I had a sudden wild impulse to jump up and grope for the light switch. Jim had sent his love to Donna, that was fine... except that he wasn't around to tell her in person anymore. I swallowed hard. It wasn't my call to make, but hers.

Persia continued in a soft monotone. "Donna, please look at the Ouija board. I am sensing that Jim wants to tell you something else. Shall we proceed?"

Donna raised her blanched face to Persia and nodded once. Our unblinking eyes riveted to the planchette again. It stood still. Dan let out a sigh and seemed about to speak when it came back to life and made its slow slide to the letter B, stopped again, then E.

I swallowed again and shifted my weight to one

side. My fingers were numbing fast. Dan's face was a study in concentration, his dark brow furrowed as his fingers touched ours. Persia had a faraway look in her eyes, the candlelight and shadow accenting her fey-otherworld appearance.

Donna's eyes were unwavering on the planchette. It stopped. I thought maybe that was as far as it would travel, with some sense of relief, but then it moved again. Mouths open in wonder, we watched unflinchingly as it paused at the letter F, then R, then E. It paused again, as if unsure of itself, moved back, then returned to the E. Be free.

A freshet of wind blew through the candles, extinguishing all but one. Donna's head slumped forward on her chest, her shadowed hair concealing her face. I jumped up to go to her, nearly tripping on my chair, when a low moan pierced the air. It escalated into a wild shrieking wail. I followed it to Winklin on the climber to my right, his lone eye fiery, head arched back, as he stared at the ceiling. The last candle went out.

Before we could do anything, the two porch windows blasted shocking white light through the downstairs. Dan charged for the front door knocking over a chair in his haste. An ear splitting, metallic crash rang outside. Donna's sweaty hands grabbed mine. We escaped from the table to follow him.

The hair from Persia's braid brushed my arm as she rushed up behind us to the open door. An ungainly trio, we baby stepped sideways along to the screen door and gingerly peeked through. Dan stood at the far side of the drive by the cedars when he swung his attention back to us. We clung to each other like frightened schoolgirls in the doorway.

"A possum, ladies!" His laugh chortled through the gloom. "No ghosts or evil spirits. Damn, they're weird looking. Must have been searching for vegan leftovers when it knocked over the garbage can and lid over there." He pointed to the side of the house. "Bet it scared the sh… crap out of him. He scuttled away so fast!" Dan was still cracking up as he made his way back to us. We let out a collective sigh of relief, then went inside to put on some lights.

—oOo—

CHAPTER TWELVE

The display on the clock flashed a searing neon 12:35 a.m. into Jessica's bleary eyes. She flung herself back onto her rumpled bed, cursing. The chill-pill she took hours earlier made her body feel drained and her throat parched. With great effort, she rolled onto her side, rubbed one eye and reached for her phone. She stared in a stupor at it. No calls. No texts. Memory hit her like an avalanche.

Dan.

Their worst fight ever.

What was to be a romantic trip to a country winery for a fine dining celebration, turned into a shitstorm by the side of a rural road. It all returned in sickening Technicolor. The anger that set her heart pounding, that terrifying moment of rage when she literally threw him out of her car. The hate she felt. It was horrible.

The disaster seemed a lifetime ago instead of just hours. She pushed herself up on the bed, straightened her leaden arms and stretched them high above her head wiggling her fingers. Gradually her bedroom came into better focus as she attempted to stand. One hand pushed her tangled hair back as the other found his number. After five rings it rolled over to voicemail. She cringed in shame as she heard his friendly greeting asking the caller to leave a message.

"I'm an idiot!" she cried out to the darkened room. "I threw his phone into the woods."

She recalled his crumpled body lying on the shoulder of the road where she had dumped him, possibly hurt, as she brutally tore away in her car. Further up the road, she'd slammed on the brakes, then, with a fury unknown to her until that terrible second, pitched his phone with all her might into the black maw of a wooded area.

She tore home with no regard to speed. It was either a few drinks or a tranq. She'd seriously considered getting totally wasted and eyed the Grey Goose, then had decided upon her handy go-to, Ativan. It would take less time to escape herself in the twilight oblivion of sleep.

She heaved a nervous sigh and shuddered as she ran her hand over dry lips. There had to be some way to connect with him tonight. What would he do? Where would he go?

Dan was no fool. He'd find some way to get back to his apartment at Rick's. Hell, he'd probably caught a ride with some old hayseed coming back from the Saturday downtown market. It was only a twenty-minute drive into town from where she'd left him. Maybe he walked some of it. But what if he couldn't? What if he was injured?

She had to get a hold of Rick. It was still early for a Saturday night. He and Dan were probably quaffing Molson's in Rick's dump of a kitchen, discussing what a screwed-up bitch she was. She would call, not text. There was no answer, so she left a voicemail asking if Dan was with him. She paced back and forth, waiting for the phone's ring, getting antsier by the second.

The room loomed dark and foreboding. Dark shapes of furniture magnified in the evening gloom. Downtown night traffic punctured the air with the rumble of engines and the blast of horns. Jessica flicked on a Limoges lamp by the door and blinked at its harsh light. It seemed like forever since they were here last. Before his interview. The job he didn't want and that she insisted would be best for him because her father said so. Well, her father didn't consider small-town musicians' career-minded people. He used other words. Words she'd never tell Dan.

Jess wandered back and forth, occasionally pausing to prop her head against the cool window to search the sidewalk four floors down, unsure of what to do next. Call the cops? They might investigate and at least rule out foul play. She stopped pacing and clutched her head with both hands. Foul play? What was she thinking? How many hours had it been? Eight hours, not twenty-four. He wouldn't even be termed a missing person. Of course Dan was fine. Upset and pissed at her, but not in danger. That was TV crap.

She jumped as her phone buzzed.

Rick.

Shivering, she hugged her chest, then answered.

"Hey, Jess. You still lookin' for Danny boy?" he shouted above a din.

There were bar sounds in the background, raucous band blare and the loud clinking of noisy drinkers. She pictured his big leering face. He would have some fun with this. She swallowed and clenched the phone with a tight fist.

"Hey, Rick. Yeah, I thought he would be at his apartment, well your place." She hesitated and bit her bottom lip, unsure of how much to give away. She knew Rick didn't like her. He'd probably be happy to hear about the fight.

"Guess you're out of luck, Jessie girl. Haven't

seen or heard nothin' from the boy. I texted him some time ago. Thought I could talk him into getting together with the guys for a bit of fun, if you know what I mean? He didn't get back to me. Figgered he was with you. Saturday night, no gig, ya know? Maybe he's on the prowl." He gave a dry, dirty laugh. "Sorry. Couldn't resist. I know you keep him on a pretty tight leash. I'll let ya know if I hear anything." He chuckled and hung up.

She squeezed her eyes shut, willing the tears away. Rick was a jerk and a troublemaker. She uttered a barely audible "Yeah," then hung up.

Maybe he was lying. Dan was at a local watering hole with him, yukking it up as they made fun of her. She imagined Rick's beady eyes lighting up with glee as Dan regaled him with his tale of Jessica-gone-psycho. She took a deep breath, then straightened her shoulders.

No. That wasn't Dan. No matter how many difficulties they had, he would be loyal to her. Even if, God forbid, they finally broke up, he had the decency not to go around bad-mouthing her. And he sure as hell wouldn't have stranded her at the side of a remote country road.

Hot, salty tears of shame slid down her face. She wiped them angrily with trembling fingers. Her stomach lurched as she stumbled to the bathroom, just making it over the toilet to wretch and sputter a yellow stream of vomit. She squinted at the mirror staring at puffy, mascara-streaked eyes, then spat into the sink and leaned over wearily to rinse the foul acid from her mouth.

What a bitch she was. Dan was like no guy she had met before, and there had been quite a few. Mostly jerks who thought she would be a good piece of ass. That's what most of them wanted in this podunk town anyway. She patted her lips dry.

He was the first guy to move beyond the obvious physical attraction between them to really get to know her. He listened to her from the first time they met, and didn't jump into giving her unwanted advice.

Dan appreciated the little things; hand holding, winking at a new outfit she modelled for him. He insisted on paying for dates, even though she knew his income was tight. He rarely complained and tried to make her happy.

So what if he didn't have the management job she wanted for him? That was his choice. It was his life, not hers. She needed to step back and let him find his way or just break it off. Her attitude had reared its ugly head before, but this time with dire consequences.

Jessica thought back to her sister, Taylor, and her own devastating regret at disowning her over their grandmother's will... the terrible fights and uncontrollable emotions that favouritism brought.

Gramma Malone had owned a stately, city home in Rosemount. The two sisters had spent many wonderful summers splashing around her kidney-shaped pool, being waited on by Milla, the French housekeeper. They entertained the old woman with their made-up plays and fantasies, much to her delight.

When they'd reached college age, she'd paid for their tuition in full and promised to leave her estate to them when she passed. Gramma Malone, her father's mother, had only one other child, a daughter, her father's sister, Doris, who died of pancreatic cancer when she was only thirty-nine.

But Gramma changed her mind. She confided this to Taylor and swore her to secrecy. Taylor would be the sole recipient of the estate, for reasons known only between them. Jessica grew into adulthood not knowing of the change. To make matters worse, her parents believed they would inherit the property. They separated and divorced before her grandmother died and the whole thing ended up being a vicious family feud soon after the funeral. Her mother and Taylor on one side, she and her dad on the other. That was five years ago. Her sister and mother moved out west, leaving Jessica to live with her father.

At the end of their final fight, before Taylor left, Jessica hissed over the phone that she never wanted to see her again. Three months later, Taylor was killed in a car crash in Alberta. Jessica realized that all the counselling in the world would never take back her words.

She would not lose Dan. She loved him more than anything. She scooped up her jacket and ran for the door, raising a silent prayer that she would find him, and that he could still love her.

—o0o—

CHAPTER THIRTEEN

The Westin Hotel's tropical themed Sand Bar was alive with buzzing conversation and a rock band onstage amping the oldies. The cat-friendly crowd was in full force, bouncing to the pulsating beat of Johnny's Juke Boxers. Lisa held her martini glass lightly while she schmoozed with a gaggle of ladies at the grass-thatched tiki bar.

The success of her presentation left her relieved and ready to party. She had managed to down three green apple vodka martinis, courtesy of her loving husband, who was enjoying his own celebration. She waved her fingers playfully at him and blew a kiss from across the room. He held up his beer bottle in a toast with a sneaky wink, mouthing the words "later."

"Well, here's our Pause for Claws member extraordinaire, Ms. Lisa Bristow!" proclaimed a deep voice.

It was the wisecracking membership chairman, Bud Michaels. He sidled up to her bar stool with a sexy wink to the ladies watching. His frosted beer mug clinked softly against her cocktail glass. Lisa giggled at his joie de vivre and leaned forward to take another sip of her delicious drink.

"Well done, Lisa. Proud owner of nine incredible felines. I want to see your cat palace next time I'm down your way. Do you train your brood to be that camera, or rather video, ready? It was good to see indoor cats able to roam outside. I especially liked the butterfly jumper, the black and white one," he smiled.

Lisa's face flushed with pride. "That was Snappy. He is quite the jumper! I'm glad I was able to catch him in midair. I spent hours just waiting for the right shot. You're welcome to visit anytime, and thank you for the compliment. The video was fun to make. It took a few weeks to get them all on there. It really does make a difference for them to get outside. I notice a few of them seem anxious if they can't be out due to bad weather."

She played with her cocktail napkin for a few seconds, then turned to him, suddenly serious.

"I couldn't have done the presentation tonight without Brad's input though. He's my rock. His creative energy inspires me, and he has a lot more patience than I do. I'm relieved it went well. I was quite nervous up there. There sure were a lot of people watching.

"I don't consider myself to be much of a public speaker, but someone told me, if you believe strongly in a cause you would fight for, then that gives you the drive to promote it any way you can. Brad reminded me, before I took the steps up to the stage, that I had nothing to worry about. Our cats are all in our beautiful new home, safe with my mom, and my presentation would be perfect. He didn't even see a run-through because I wanted him to watch it all for the first time tonight!"

Bud smiled again, displaying even, white teeth, his horn-rims a deep black in the table light. He gave her a victory sign, then turned his attention to someone at the bar.

"Well, congrats again!" He touched her shoulder and moved around a server balancing a trayful of shots into the hot swarm of people.

A statuesque brunette, nails dripping scarlet polish, dramatically swept up to in a blaze of red chiffon.

"Lisa," she purred as she slid a long tawny arm around her.

It was Dinah Costoff, a long-time supporter of Pause for Claws and a well-known animal activist in the Toronto area.

"Dinah!" Lisa slid off her stool to embrace the

glamourous woman. A rich exotic fragrance of ylang-ylang hung in the air between them.

"I haven't seen you in ages," Lisa gushed. "You always look ready for the runway." She stepped back to admire Dinah's evening wear.

"Oh, Lisa. You're always so sweet. Thank you. I've just returned from Bermuda, and I'm so happy I didn't miss this event. I brought my friend Eduardo de Finca over to meet you."

A swarthy, European looking gentleman with a grey goatee took Lisa's hand and held it to his lips to kiss.

"Honoured to meet you," he said, his smile brilliant. "I was very impressed with your presentation. You have your hands full. Nine cats. I hope you have help with litter detail. That's a lot of kitty do-do!"

Dinah hooted with laughter, then pulled his face to hers for a quick smooch.

Lisa blushed at this intimacy. She took another quick sip from her glass, returning to her topic of the evening.

"Another good reason to invest in safety fencing. Although I have to say, they still use the litter boxes inside more than the outdoors. Old habits die hard, I guess."

Dinah's remarkable green eyes sparkled over her highball.

"So, Lisa, can we expect an update on the cat fence in the new location? Maybe more kitties, too?" she said.

"Well…" Lisa pushed back a lock of hair that had fallen forward. She moved closer, about to confide something to her friend, when Brad appeared at her shoulder.

"I heard that, Dinah." Brad mocked a stern frown. "Nine is enough, especially with the one-eyed villain we have. That one bears watching!" He hugged his wife to his side.

"That's Winklin." she giggled. "My mom calls him Winky. He can be a little devil, always after Nukkers, when he can find her. I think he just wants to play with a smaller kitty. I just love him to bits!"

Lisa glanced around the boisterous crowd as Brad and the others continued their conversation. Marsha had cornered Selma near the doors to the restrooms, or perhaps it was the other way around. They had their heads together, deep in serious conversation. It might be about Muriel.

Selma, ever the fashionista, was striking in an Amazon-style, slinky black mini dress. Lisa thought it was a bit youthful for a woman pushing fifty. Perhaps the *sexy, tough, career woman* was her signature look. She'd heard a rumour that Selma had work done on her face, then dropped the poor schmuck who paid for it the year before.

Whatever her style, Lisa wasn't impressed by Selma's hard-driven business persona. How could that ever be better than Muriel's natural ability to relate to people from all walks of life? Muriel was proud of her age and didn't have to resort to treatments. No way would the plastic Selma be a better director than Muriel. There were so many long-time members who would stand by the classy, older director.

Lisa scanned the room to see if she could spot Muriel's gorgeous upswept hair while members chatted and milled around. She finally caught sight of her at the far end of the bar by a fake-looking palm tree. Muriel had her back to her, holding treasurer Jay Breedlove's arm, their heads close as they spoke. Jay stood next to Sacha Wachter who was in charge of public relations. They broke into sudden laughter, apparently at something Jay remarked, wildly gesticulating with his hand.

It seemed strange to Lisa that Muriel held a wine glass. She knew the woman couldn't drink alcohol because of her medication for high blood pressure. She'd confided to Lisa that her doctor had started her on a new medication as the previous prescription made her nauseous. No, her drink would be non-alcoholic, possibly Perrier. There was no way Muriel would compromise this high-profile annual event.

Marsha broke away from Selma, making for the ebullient bar crowd where the director stood. Lisa's breath caught as she felt a rush of protection. What if Marsha was going to confront Muriel? She took another gulp of her drink. The band sounded louder, more distracting than entertaining. Why were people talking so loudly? She couldn't think straight.

"Honey, what can I get you?" Brad startled Lisa. She swivelled in her seat to see him nursing the same beer.

"Huh? Oh, I'm okay for now." She kept her eyes on Marsha, who was now hailing a table of strangers motioning her over to them.

"Can I ask you something?" Lisa's gaze followed the broad back of the swaying social convenor.

He took a pull from his beer, wiping the foam from his moustache with the back of his hand.

"Of course. What's up, babe? You're not still worried about the cats, are you?"

She looked down at her drink, pursed her lips, then drew close to him and whispered, "Brad, did you know that some members of the board are trying to get rid of Muriel? Marsha's quite excited about the whole thing. I bet she's one of them."

He paused, looking over to the bar as if searching for Marsha.

"I didn't want to say anything at this point. It's a rumour. Nothing is definite. Marsha happens to be friendly with Selma. No conspiracy there. It may seem like it though. Selma's quite opinionated and has no compunction in expressing her views to anyone, not just Marsha. You have to remember, hon, there's politics in every high-profile organization, even the do-gooder ones." He gave a short laugh. "They may be the worst. It boils down to money. Whoever can bring in the most and use it effectively. I've heard Selma Daniels is interested in the position. Ever think our fearless leader may be ready to move over?"

A loud shout interrupted them.

"Brad! Lisa! Hey, over here!" A familiar, gray-haired couple waved them over to offer a couple of seats at their table.

It was Charlie Drake and his wife, Claire, from Etobicoke. Charlie had been on the board in his younger years, but packed it in after a stroke scare. The barrel-chested country boy was fondly called *old reliable* because he rarely missed a board meeting.

Brad hailed them and steered Lisa in their

direction. He bent over and confided to her on the way.

"Charlie will know what's going on with Muriel. You know him. He shoots from the hip. Let's see what's up."

"Hey, guys!" Charlie and Claire slid their chairs over to make room for the young couple. Lisa was jostled to one side by a frazzled female server balancing a precarious tray. Brad caught Lisa by the waist and pulled her to him, as Charlie called for drinks from another server barely keeping up the pace. Lisa declined and sat, happy to see the excited Claire. It had been some time since they had chatted.

"Lisa, you were great up there! Ever thought of public speaking as a career?" she asked, her eyes bright and mischievous.

She reminded Lisa of the actress Kathy Bates.

"I wouldn't have the nerve to do that in front of the hoi polloi of cat charities," Claire continued, taking Lisa's hand.

"It was way worse waiting to go up on stage," Lisa said. "I had butterflies in my tummy. Once I got into the story of our kitties and their great personalities, I felt better. The laughter of the audience and their applause gave me so much energy, like an adrenaline rush. I kept thinking, these people are cat lovers just like me. We have this incredible bond."

"Well, I could tell you were having fun with it, and that's the main thing, right? It's a great cause and a special night out. This whole evening has been lovely. Charlie and I were really looking forward to it. And," she preened, "it gave me a chance to get out of my jeans and into something fancy."

"Oh, you're so right, Claire. I don't dress up much, especially working from home. I do love that lime green on you. It picks up the highlights in your hair." Lisa looked across the table to see her husband kidding around with Charlie, slapping the husky man's shiny, brown back. His gruff voice carried over to the ladies.

"The old girl might have shot herself in the foot with that crazy speech blooper. Senior moment?" he guffawed. "Heard she's had a lot of those lately!"

Brad flashed an anxious look at Lisa.

"Don't listen to Charlie." Claire protested. "He's had plenty of brain farts. Why I bet he couldn't tell you what he had for breakfast this morning. We all have those moments, senior or not." She frowned, then changed the subject.

"So, you're a country girl now, eh? That must be lovely for you both. Peaceful surroundings with the lure of going back to nature." Her hazel eyes twinkled.

"You know, Lisa, I grew up on a farm in Listowel. That's where my love of cats began. At one point my brothers and sisters and I had fifteen. Mind you, they were barn cats, but we named them all, and they did keep the mouse population down. It was a great place to grow up. My folks had fifty acres for crops and livestock. We had all kinds of farm animals – horses, cows, chickens, white geese. As a kid, I insisted on..." Her thoughts ceased as her attention diverted to the dance floor.

"Oh, look, Lisa!" she pointed, "Muriel's shaking her booty with some of the younger ladies. What fun. She is so spry. You'd never know she's in her seventies."

Lisa pushed closer to Claire for a better look. It was hard for her to see Muriel with all the revellers' glittering heads bobbing to the band's rocking rendition of Bob Seger's "Old Time Rock 'n Roll." Then she spotted Muriel's silver updo and flailing bejewelled arms above the crowd. The woman was certainly whooping it up. Lisa was somewhat taken aback by her behaviour. It seemed quite over the top for the normally sedate woman. She looked away from the dance area to see if Brad noticed, but he was busy talking to Charlie and Claire.

A loud cry, much like an animal's, tore through the music's blare. The frantic dancing faltered then died as people slid back from the centre of the dance floor while the band continued to rock. Lisa scanned the area desperately to see what had happened.

No sign of Muriel.

With a low cry, Lisa broke away from their table and pushed through the sea of bodies toward the stage. A hysterical keening split the air. Breathless, Lisa forged to the edge of the onlookers and froze. She stared open-mouthed at the bizarre tableau before her.

Muriel was writhing about on the floor in a froth of blue satin, grappling with a smaller red-haired woman wearing a black dress. They were thrashing their arms about trying to get a grasp on each other like drug-crazed lovers. When the reddened, distorted face of the woman in black turned toward Lisa, she saw with horror it was Selma Daniels.

"You little conniver!" Muriel spat, her mouth a snarling gash, the once perfect silver coif spilling wildly from its French twist.

"Let me go, Muriel!" the younger woman screeched, fiercely wrenching herself away. One of her patent stiletto heels skidded across the floor. She drove a desperate claw into the director's apoplectic face. Muriel jerked her cheek away, then in one swift, never to be forgotten movement, clung to Selma's single silk shoulder strap and tore it down. The dress's bra snapped off, exposing Selma's large freckled breasts.

The guitar playing singer clearly enjoyed the impromptu striptease. He gave a whistling catcall and winked at the struggling duo.

"Well, ladies and gents," he dragged the mike closer and announced to the horrified semi-circle. "Looks like we have a real catfight on our hands!" Chuckling, he wiggled his lean hips, then broke into a rocking rendition of "Cat Scratch Fever."

Marsha jostled her way to the front of the onlookers, another woman at her heels. They grabbed Muriel's struggling arms, peeling her off the younger woman, then gripped her between them. Someone flung a man's black dinner jacket over Selma and helped her to stand, putting a protective arm around her. The woman's pretty face was marred by shock and embarrassment. She scowled at Muriel, charging forward to retaliate, when Muriel bawled at her, spittle foaming her mouth.

"You'll never take over my position, Selma! Never! I will, I will..." she slurred, her eyes widened in two blue pools, then rolled back into her head. Her large limp body sagged forward and fell into the arms of the speechless Bud Michaels.

"Call 911," he cried. With help from Marsha and some other spectators, he gently guided the director down to a prone position.

Lisa called out for Brad, who stood transfixed behind her. He didn't move.

"Oh my God!" she gasped as the buzz in the room grew around them like a swarm of insects. She clung to his jacket; her body wracked in sobs.

"Brad, what has happened to Muriel? I can't believe this. She's possessed or something. She can't drink. She wouldn't. I know she wouldn't. Someone did this to her. They drugged her Perrier. This is terrible. She's made a spectacle of herself on the very evening she worked all year for. It will kill her. I feel sick..."

Brad held her close and murmured to calm her as the band took a welcome break. Some of the shocked cat crowd made a beeline to the bar and their tables. A hotel employee, his face unflinching with the task at hand, arrived laden with Hudson's Bay blankets to cover Muriel who was now splayed out on the floor, one exquisite blue Jimmy Choo fallen by her foot.

Guests moved in clusters to break away from the tawdry scene. A steady hum of gossip filled the air.

Words like "drunk," "drugs," and "nervous breakdown" were whispered in hushed tones as the guests surveyed the scene.

Charlie came rushing up to them, his brown eyes wide in disbelief, ample belly leading the way. "What the hell! What happened out there?"

Claire came over to Lisa's side, putting a plump arm around her. She spoke in a soothing voice. "This is so sad honey. I can't believe it. I've known Muriel... we have, for years."

Charlie nodded, his gray comb-over rakish as he wiped the sweat off his forehead with a large, white handkerchief.

"This place is hotter than hell," he muttered. "Let's get some fresh air. What a shitshow."

"Honey, watch your language." Claire ordered him, with a quick look to Lisa.

They moved away from the disaster to a divan in a lobby chat area, relieved to get out of the Sand Bar. A siren blared from the highway and, before they spoke again, two paramedics rushed through the main lobby entrance pushing a stretcher holding black cases of equipment. A few stragglers made way for them to pass through.

Brad moved back in his seat and put an arm around Lisa. He dragged a tired hand over his face, then spoke in a low tone to the others.

"This is one helluva screw up for Pause for Claws. I know I'm stating the obvious. I mean, I hope Muriel is okay of course, but this will have repercussions, maybe a lawsuit."

Charlie sat across from them holding Claire's hand. He looked at them soberly.

"I know you're very close to her, Lisa," he said. "No one knew, but I'm thinking that Muriel's private stress led to this. It was very drastic, but people do strange things when they feel they are losing control of something vital to them. Maybe she took something to relax herself before she came here tonight. We may never know." He gave a sad look to his wife.

Lisa stared at her hands, lying limp like dead birds in her lap. Brad took one, rubbing it slowly. "I think it's time to get some shut-eye, eh Lise? It's been a long day and, hopefully, things will be better tomorrow after a night's rest."

He rose from his seat to give Claire a hug. She reached up to rub his back, casting a worried glance at Lisa, then waved to her and called out good night. Charlie offered his hand to Brad and he shook it. Brad watched them stroll slowly toward the far elevators, Charlie with a solicitous arm around Claire's ample waist.

Lisa, still on the divan, gazed up at her husband's thoughtful face. She knew Brad was very knowledgeable about people and their quirks. He'd seen a lot of strange behaviours due to alcohol in his job at the L.C.B.O. over the years. Right now, he looked to be a million miles away.

She tugged at his jacket. The motion broke his thoughts as he looked down at her.

"What are you thinking?" she asked, her eyes dark moons, as she gripped his hand hard. "Brad. What if Muriel goes into a coma? or worse! I think we should stay here with her."

He frowned at her suggestion, then put a big hand on her shoulder.

"She'll be all right. We can't do anything for her right now. It's scary for sure, but she'll get the help she needs at the hospital. We can only surmise what happened here tonight and what will happen as a result of this mess. I would bet my money Charlie's right. Muriel got into the sauce out of stress. She must have known for some time that Selma was after her position. It worked on her nerves. She didn't want anyone to know, especially you, honey. Hiding anxiety eventually disrupts our health. We don't know much about Muriel's personal life either. There may have been other things that were causing her pain."

Brad grasped Lisa's cold hand and gently led her down the plush carpeted hallway to the twin elevators. He guided her forward as the stainless-steel doors swished open.

"They'll take care of her. She's out cold. Maybe a good thing before she did further damage." He pressed the button for the fifth floor. "She was pretty rough on Selma. All Muriel needs is an assault charge thrown at her."

They watched the red numbers flash up to their floor uninterrupted. Brad turned to her.

"Muriel has always been a tower of strength and self-control. The unexpected can happen anywhere to anyone. I'm sure we'll hear about it tomorrow. I hope it doesn't affect the fundraising tonight. That sounds cold, I know, but you know what people are like. It's late and I'm ready to crash. We'll have a good sleep, some breakfast, and head home first thing in the morning."

"It's just so strange," Lisa mused. "Like something went weird in her brain. But I still think someone did something to her. I just bet Selma orchestrated this to have Muriel make a fool of herself!"

Brad smiled. "Ah Lisa, I think you've been reading too many mystery novels. Though it is an interesting thought. Could a person want directorship of a volunteer organization that badly?"

A quiet ching announced their floor as the doors slid back to reveal a chic couple of twenty-somethings locked in a hot embrace. They appeared unabashed to be caught groping. The girl snickered as they slid into the elevator. Lisa sighed and put her head on Brad's bicep as the elevator doors closed. Within minutes they were in their room and under the covers.

"Two things about Muriel's catastrophe tonight," Brad reflected as he reached over to turn off their bedside lamp.

Lisa inched closer to him, snuggling into the warmth of his soft beard. He smelled of peppermint toothpaste and Nautica.

"What's that?" she slurred in a sleepy voice.

"It's distracted you from kitty worry." His words hung in the darkened room. She gave his arm a firm squeeze and huffed back on her pillow.

"I'm still a bit worried, but we haven't heard anything. And Mom doesn't like texting, so I decided to stop bugging her with mine. She would let me know if there was anything wrong. And really, what could go wrong in twenty-four hours? We've been gone for thirteen and a half of them already. She's probably catching up on gossip, not even thinking to check for messages. They don't get together often. I'll be glad to get home. I hope Muriel's okay."

She flipped onto her side, paused, then rolled back to touch his arm.

"Wait. You said two things."

"Oh yeah," he muttered softly into her hair, then cleared his throat.

"Selma does have nice tits," he murmured.

"Bradley!" She pulled his beard hard. "I didn't think you liked freckles." She giggled.

He uttered a hearty laugh, hugging her to his chest.

—o0o—

CHAPTER FOURTEEN

Rubbing his chilled hands together for circulation, Dan made a straight line for the Barca lounger by the fireplace and collapsed with a loud groan. Donna and Persia plunked themselves opposite him, a pair of worn-out rag dolls, their blonde and gray heads lolling against the sofa cushions, half-lidded eyes ready for sleep.

We had decided to calm ourselves after the seance/possum scare with hot cups of Persia's chamomile sleepy tea, while Dan selected a Molson's nightcap.

I covered my mouth to suppress a sudden yawn, then walked over to sit on the red retro chair that had become my favourite. It was time to get ready for bed.

"Sorry, Dan, but I don't think I'm in any shape to get you home," I confessed. "I've been drinking on and off all afternoon and I may fall asleep at the wheel. You're welcome to crash here on the sofa or please feel free to call a cab or Uber."

He smiled, then wiped his hair back from his brow.

"Hey, no problem, Reggie. I'm good with a cab, but you'll have to do the calling." He held empty hands up.

I waved him off. "Of course I will. Just relax and finish your beer."

Persia opened her sleepy eyes to him and sighed. "I'm sorry too, Dan. I know I told you I would get you home, but I couldn't drive even if I wanted to. I need recharging. Seances can be very draining." She removed her wire rims, massaging the narrow bridge of her nose. "What an interesting evening. I would never have predicted a night like this."

Donna straightened a cushion on the sofa, then stroked Winky's long thick fur, much to his pleasure. He arched his back and rubbed sensuously against her thigh.

I got up and moved around, collecting the remaining empty mugs.

"A night I will never forget." Donna exhaled wistfully as she stretched catlike, massaging her elbows. Winky leaped off the sofa in an orange and white blur. He proceeded to sniff out his little pal Hermie, who was dozing spread-eagled on the back of Dan's recliner.

"Aside from Dan's possum heroics," Donna admitted. "The scariest part of this evening was contacting Jim for his final message, then seeing the porch light up right after. Like he was at the door. I freaked!"

"Me too," I said. "It's spooky in this old place when it's only lit by candlelight. My nerves are still buzzing. Well, now I can say I have been to my first seance and it was... Oh shit!"

I clapped a hand to my mouth, remembering my earlier promise to Lisa.

Persia shifted from her repose; her eyes now wide.

"What Reggie? What happened?" She looked sleepily around the room.

"Damn. I forgot to get back to Lisa. It's been hours! Though it doesn't seem like it. I'm actually afraid to check my phone to see all her frantic messages. If she only knew about our impromptu party this afternoon, and spirit-raising adventure this evening."

I stopped and eyeballed the three of them. "Which she won't." I threatened, drawing a finger across my throat.

Dan took a swig of his beer and made a big gesture of crossing his heart.

"Secret's safe with me Reggie. I don't expect I'll

ever meet your daughter and son-in-law anyway, so I wouldn't be tempted to squeal. It's kind of weird how things happen, you know? I had a really awesome time today. Like, totally unexpected. Who knew that I'd have these experiences tonight because of a chance encounter at the side of a country road?" He laughed. "Not even you, Madam Fortune Teller!"

Persia crimsoned.

Crossing his arms over his chest, Dan observed his dark reflection in the window. "Well, it got my mind off my troubles, for a while anyway. I don't want to go back to reality."

After a few beats of awkward silence, I ventured, "I think you mean Jessica."

I watched his expression in the glass, wondering if I was too bold in mentioning her name. He turned his face from its reflection and looked at me, letting out a long sigh.

"Yeah, Jessica." He licked beer foam from his moustache and went on, his voice dull in confession. "I need to make some changes in my life."

Another long silence.

Donna was checking her phone. "It's after midnight, Reggie. I bet Lisa and Brad are sleeping after a busy day. Maybe you shouldn't call or you'll wake them."

I nodded at her suggestion, and decided to send a quick reassuring text message instead.

Persia roused herself to wander toward the kitchen, her bare feet padding softly toward an area rug. The snick of the fridge door opening accompanied her talking to one of the cats. At least, I hoped it was a cat.

"Oh, I don't know if they'll get much sleep, Donna. This was a big night for them. They don't go out often. They say they're too tired, but this event would provide lots of networking for Lisa. She's either on the phone or the computer with members. Of course, her idol, the queen bee, Mrs. Muriel Peabody will be there. Lisa loves her to pieces. She may be too excited to sleep..." My voice faded as I grunted, and moved forward to slide my hand down the side of the chair. I couldn't feel my phone.

"Where is my phone anyway?" I asked the others. I went around the room checking as I spoke. "There are too many places here to lose track of things."

Dan stretched his long arm over and with an easy hand slid some decorating magazines aside on an overburdened end table. He handed me my red cell phone.

"Definitely not mine," he said.

I thanked him, then looked at the screen, unsure of

how to proceed. Lisa could be difficult, especially when she was tired or overwrought. I wasn't in the mood for histrionics. I could say something she would misconstrue, causing trouble. Brad had a way with her. He was able to maintain clear thinking in any situation, the perfect match for Lisa's nervous nature. I was sure he would talk her into going to bed and putting concerns about the cats to rest. I'd simply ignore her many texts and forge ahead with my own message. She would see it first thing in the morning. It would be something apologetic, to ease her mind about the cats. Something like,

Lisa, I'm sorry for not getting back to you sooner. Everything is fine and we're off to bed.

I started the text.

Lisa I'm sorry

A sharp gasp of breath froze my fingers with Persia's cry from the kitchen.

"I see it!" she hollered, panicked. I looked up from the phone. She stood on the other side of the pass-through, her head haloed by a night light.

Please, God, not another spirit. I dropped the phone on my chair and ran to the kitchen. Her face was a rictus of horror, eyes riveted to the dining room.

"I see a fire!" she shrilled, pointing to the tall darkened windows.

Donna and Dan jumped up from their seats and ran to the dining room. The shed was on fire. Quick little flames danced along the edges of its dark doorway. I fled back to my phone to call 911, while the others jammed through the front door.

"Garden hose, side of the house, hurry! Opposite the shed!" I barked out the orders. Scooping my phone off the chair, I punched in the emergency numbers and called out information to the dispatcher.

Outside, Dan frantically uncoiled the green hose from its plastic roller. He gripped the nozzle, desperately jerking his arms to pull the hose free. Donna had found a shovel and was digging up dirt from the side garden to throw at the flames. The shed's interior belched plumes of acrid smoke. The hose kinked. Dan swore. I raced over to untangle it. We managed to get it within fifteen feet of the shed when a stream of cold water finally gushed out. His wet hands shook as he trained it on the shed roof and tried to saturate where it attached to the garage. The hose sputtered, then sprayed hard again.

I stumbled over to the rusty faucet and turned the handle as far as it would go. Lisa and Brad were on cistern; I hoped the water didn't run out. Again, the water stream strengthened. Dan moved in closer to train it on the garage roof. If the firefighters didn't arrive soon, it would be next. We needed more water, now.

Dan was shouting something, his eyes two dark pits in his face.

"Reggie? Reggie! No cars in the garage, right?" He was pleading. I held a plastic wash bucket, about to fill it from the pond, when I jerked to a stop. My stomach spasmed and I almost retched.

"Lisa's Lexus!" I cried, shocked that I hadn't thought of it sooner. I threw the pail and spun around recklessly to go back into the house for the remote. Donna followed close behind. We shoved our dinner dishes aside, eyes scouring the countertops. I spotted the fob beside the toaster, grabbed it, and dashed out.

Dan waved the limp hose valiantly, but the puny spring that spewed out was no match for the blaze. Searing flames crackled and lit up the night as the fire edged toward the eaves of the garage.

Brad's caution about the remote came to me as I stood shaking before the wide door. My hands felt like icicles despite the heat surging from the buildings in waves. The remote slipped from my trembling hand before I could use it. I cursed and wiped my blurry eyes with a shirt cuff. Donna bent quickly to retrieve it and passed it to me.

Grasping it hard, I said a silent prayer, then

pressed. A low mechanical hum rose as the metal door began its slow ascent. Welcome sounds of sirens echoed in the distance. Lisa's car would be safe. The garage door came to an abrupt halt halfway up.

"Here! Give it to me!" Dan ordered.

Taking the remote from my hand, he pushed at the pad, with desperate fingers. The door would not move. Again, and again, he mashed at the pad, gritting his teeth in frustration.

"Aw, shit!" he cried out and flung it to the ground.

"Come on. Maybe we can push it up!" I made my way through the thickening smoke.

I'd try anything to get that damn car out. Dan and Donna were close behind, gasping. Dan cursed a blue streak. Behind us, a familiar voice broke through the chaos. I peered back. Persia's breathless figure ran toward us, her right hand extended.

"Give me the opener!" she demanded.

I wanted to pick it up and throw it at her.

"Where the hell have you been?" I growled at her. "It won't work! You can help us push this goddamn door up!"

Muttering under my breath, I returned to my efforts to wedge my shoulder beneath the door. Donna was breathing hard as we cursed the mechanism with each push.

Dan shrugged, then scooped the remote from the gravel. He tossed it to Persia. She caught it awkwardly with both hands.

"Okay, gypsy lady, let's see what you can do. I say the car is toast!" He moved back to his work, angrily bashing the door with his fists.

"Freeze!" Persia ordered, the glint of flames lighting her face. "Everyone step away from the door!" she commanded.

Her voice was deep, harsh, like an angry man's. The little girl lilt was gone.

"Back away, I said!" she barked, motioning with the broken door opener like it was a revolver. Damp tunics hung like dirty, wet rags on her skeletal frame.

We moved back from the taunting door, reluctantly resigned to whatever ridiculous ritual Persia was about to perform. The sirens were close now, a steely scream in the black of night. She held the remote high above her taut, trembling body and uttered a soft incantation, then repeated it increasingly louder. I thought she had lost her mind.

"Elaud! Elaud! Great all-seeing one! Do my will, do my will, I humbly ask of thee." Her face shone scarlet, the plea feverish in the blaze of firelight. Sweat ran down our dirty faces as we grimly watched her click the security pad.

Like a servant summoned to perform a duty, the motor thrummed once again. The door resumed its slow, humming rise until a gaping hole exposed the waiting black Lexus. We surged forward, tripping over ourselves in blind haste to the car.

Dan scrambled in, moved something down by the shifter and slotted it into neutral, his arm wrenching hard with the effort. He turned, grabbed the driver door frame, and dug in his heels. Donna and Persia rushed to the rear of the car, leaning in to push, while I manned the passenger side, clutching the door frame. A loud sucking swoosh in the rafters heralded a heavy wave of heat. The fire had mushroomed into the garage.

Dan hollered, "We only have seconds! Count of three, push forward, pull back, forward, then pull back. We'll get this bitch out of here. One, two, three. Push!"

Breathing hard, he bent his head to the task. Across the seats from him, I wrapped my fingers around the doorframe and sent my weight forward, my runners pitted against the concrete floor. We pushed the Lexus forward, then it yielded enough for us to pull it back. With a strength I never thought possible, we rocked it and got it going forward. Gradually, it gained momentum.

We cheered as we maneuvered it out to the driveway. In the clear, some fifty feet away, we collapsed across the warm hood of the car, our lungs and bodies spent. We watched as with a whooshing roar, the space where the Lexus sat only moments before engulfed in flames.

Persia started a harsh, dry cough, her body bending over with the effort. Smoke billowed in gray clouds from the garage opening.

"Well done, ladies." Dan coughed, rubbing his streaming eyes.

Piercing white light suddenly shot up the winding drive. I was never so happy to see any sight in my life.

—oOo—

CHAPTER FIFTEEN

The first fire truck jerked to a screeching stop across from the burning buildings. Four uniformed men in safety yellow spilled out and unloaded equipment. A tall, grizzled man, replete in big overalls and a reflective helmet, lumbered over to us, clutching a worn clipboard.

"Hey, folks. I'm Captain Cal Hiskin with our local volunteer department. Are you all okay? Just you guys here?" he asked, his eyes roaming over us, then looking to the house. His broad face blanched in the lights of the nearby truck.

"No, I mean yes, just the four of us," I answered, watching him write something down. He started to speak again, but my attention shifted. All the commotion was so distracting. A pumper unit bounced along the driveway pulling up behind the first truck, the paramedics' ambulance followed. More sirens and flashers. A police car drove up and idled opposite the pergola. It mirrored a scene from a disaster movie, which I supposed in a grim way, it was. A disaster.

The fire brigade took over swiftly from our meagre attempts to put out the flames. We were now spectators, which I was relieved for. A massive hose unfolded like a sleek black cobra from the side of the pumper. It gushed forth a steady flow of water, saturating the collapsed garage roof. The crew worked diligently spraying a wide arc over the remains. Runnels of dirty water streamed from what was left of the walls, flowing onto the gravel.

I massaged my throbbing back while making a quick survey of our own crew; four bedraggled souls, dripping a mixture of soot, sweat, and hose water. We propped ourselves against the Lexus and watched as the firefighters quelled the blaze.

"Hey, Carson! Over here!" one of the young firefighters was shouting. A lengthy extension ladder rose from the back of the first truck with a grinding noise. The hose shot a torrent of water over the burning garage shingles.

I took a deep breath, while clenching my hands. I turned again to the captain. His black eyes penetrated under bushy gray brows as he looked at me expectantly, then frowned. I got back to the present in a hurry.

"I'm sorry. Yes, just the four of us," I stammered. "It's not our place. I mean it's my daughter and son-in-law's home." I was barely able to get the words out, my teeth chattered like loose dentures.

Donna put a comforting arm around my shoulders as Dan came forward.

"Hi, captain. I'm Dan Riverton and these ladies are Persia Orly and Donna Cairns. We are friends of Reggie Bristow here, and we came over for dinner. After we ate, we were talking in the living room at the back of the house. When Persia went into the kitchen, she saw a fire in the shed."

The captain faced me. "Okay, Reggie. Where are your daughter and son-in-law?"

My words sounded repetitious, like someone worn out from repeating a police statement. I thought I had already explained.

"Lisa and Brad left at noon today, I mean earlier, to attend a weekend cat conference in Toronto." I felt dizzy and disoriented. None of this was making sense.

The captain stared at me like I was on something. I desperately wanted to run away from him and forget all of this. The last taunting licks of pale flame taunted me from the smouldering walls. I didn't want to talk to anyone.

The old shed we had joked about earlier had been

reduced to nothing. A stubborn wisp of smoke rose lazily from its ashes. Next to it, dirty rivulets of water ran down the garage door, which remarkably still hung from its blackened support, a monument to mock our earlier struggle to get it open. I thanked God we were able to get Lisa's car out and no one was hurt, though I knew I'd be hurting in a number of ways tomorrow.

The thought of trying to explain this to Lisa and Brad sickened me. Lisa's first reaction would be to blame me, not for the fire but for my lack of diligence in keeping on top of everything. In other words, I had failed her. Thankfully, she wouldn't know about our shenanigans while they were away, but the thought of their coming arrival filled me with dread. My mind would teem with myriad explanations before I actually faced them. I envisioned Lisa dropping in a dead faint when they came home to this. It wasn't an exaggeration to think she could be traumatized and require sedation at the hospital.

Captain Cal spoke with Dan and Donna. He produced a small, well-thumbed notebook and bit his bottom lip in concentration, working his pen. I took a deep breath and snapped to it. It wasn't my fault. He wasn't accusing me of anything. I walked over to them.

"Excuse me, captain?" I interrupted his note-taking. "Please forgive me for not being more cooperative. I'm grateful no one was hurt and that the house is safe. I do feel a sense of guilt. Maybe it's the shock. There was nothing any of us did that could have started the fire."

I looked to Donna, who nodded her encouragement as I continued. "We explored the shed and garage in the afternoon, as this is a new home for the kids. They moved in only three weeks ago. None of us used a lighter at any time in the afternoon or evening, we were busy inside the house. I have no idea how this could have happened."

My cold hands kept clenching and unclenching at my sides. The reek of wet smoke made me ill. Captain Cal quit writing, his big freckled hands dropping to his sides.

"Look, ma'am, Reggie, think of it this way. What if no one was here overnight to call in the fire? It could have been much worse. There's a lot of dead wood in some of the trees closest to the house. It could have caught fire, then spread to the house. I'm not searching for the cause of the fire. Just the facts, ma'am, like Joe Friday. Remember that old television show, *Dragnet*?

"Fire Prevention will come out later to do an

investigation. Not all fires are sourced you know, but things have to be ruled out. The insurance company will require a copy of the investigation, assuming there is insurance?" He arched an eyebrow at me.

I nodded quickly.

"I have sent the paramedics away. Nothing for them to do here, thankfully, and Dave Jefferson, the police officer in that car over there, will be in touch with the owners once he receives documentation. Fires can start and spread in many ways. Especially in old buildings. And, we have had a dry spell for weeks. You did all the right stuff. It is a shock. We see it all the time, but that doesn't make it any easier for us. We'll do a three-sixty-degree property check around the house and any other buildings before we leave."

An insistent jerk on my right arm swung me around fast. Persia had materialized beside me, looking like a deranged clown. Her eyes bulged from a grime streaked face; her long braids twisted together in a blackened knot.

"For God's sake, Persia! What's wrong with you?" I demanded. Our group had backed over to one side as if seeing her for the first time. She recoiled from my anger, then held a shaking hand to the front of the house, tripping on her words. "The cats, Reggie! Lisa's cats. The doors. They're open!"

—oOo—

CHAPTER SIXTEEN

My head swivelled around in disbelief. The box-strewn porch was lit up like a crime scene, the screen door sagging open, swinging softly in the cool night air. The inside door teased, with a wide-open mouth, confirming our hasty exit to the fire. Illuminated like a backdrop, the kitchen and dining room showed no sign of cats. In the urgency of the fire, I hadn't even thought of them.

Captain Cal was saying something, waving his clipboard, as I spun away, tearing back to the house with Donna and Persia right behind. Dan called out something about getting a flashlight from the firefighters and checking for any cats outside.

We burst through the doorway, and I made sure to shut the door tightly behind us. Persia and Donna ran around the main floor, bumping into each other in panic. I held up my hands for a time out.

"Wait, you two! We're gonna scare them. Listen, let's do this." I put my arm around Donna. "You can be the den mother. Go around this floor, checking every possible nook and cranny that a cat could hide in and even some they couldn't. We'll take the upstairs and search the bedrooms, landing and attic. There's lots of cardboard containers and totes around for hiding places. I'm hoping they were all too freaked out by the sirens to make a run for it."

Persia crouched on the landing, groping under a velour sectional as I arrived breathless beside her.

"All the rooms across the hall, cuz, closets too." My mind raced with thoughts of possible cat hiding places up there. They were so used to quiet they may have dashed up these stairs, or even the ones to the third-floor attic when all hell broke loose.

"Persia?" I called back to her. She regarded me from the first doorway, her face anxious.

"I'm sorry for tearing your head off outside. I shouldn't take it out on you. Shout if you find any cats and we'll put them in the master bedroom. Then we'll join Dan to search outside."

She nodded solemnly and entered the closest bedroom.

I made my way to the spacious master. Flicking the light switch, I scanned the room, then checked the bathroom. Poor old Montana huddled behind the toilet, his eyes two glowing orbs. A few gentle strokes under his chin and my soft words seemed to calm him. I bent low to look under the king-sized bed, but there was nothing to see. The closets on either side of it were empty too. Persia's voice echoed from the hallway.

"Reggie! There are two kitties in the little bedroom. They look so scared behind the mattress. Should we try to get them to come out? I couldn't see anymore in here or in the other two bedrooms."

I followed her swishing skirts back to the tiny bedroom. A floral daybed propped against one windowed wall, ready to be set up. I squatted, my knee protesting as I peered around the edge of the twin mattress. Snappy clawed his way to the top, with little gray Hermie cowering behind him.

I turned away from them to face Persia.

"We should probably keep them here. I did want them all in one big room to be on the safe side, but you're right, they are frightened. Three found, six to go." I sighed, closing the door quietly. "There's an attic with a narrow staircase on the landing. I haven't been up there because Lisa told me it was creepy and they don't plan to use it, but we should check."

I led her across the landing to the front of the house. Flashes of red and blue from trucks in the driveway lit up the oak ceiling beams. We peered up the dark stairway to the third level.

I was reluctant to go forward. Lisa's words about it being haunted returned to me. Jim's earlier seance visit didn't help. I gulped, my breath quickening.

"What is it?" Persia touched my arm and stared at me, her blue eyes vigilant. "Are you afraid to go up there?"

I guffawed at her suggestion and reached my shaking hand out to take the wooden bannister.

"Who me? Of course I'm not afraid." I touched the toe of my runner to the first step.

"Well, it's okay if you are," she said sagely. "Maybe you have some psychic ability too. Attics are well known for housing spirits."

I wheeled around halfway up and caught myself before losing my balance.

"No more spirit talk! Let's get this over with. Here, take my hand." I reached behind me and felt her sweaty fingers grasp mine.

After eight cautious steps up, I abutted the smooth surface of a door. I reached down with my right hand, fumbling for the knob when I discovered the door was not closed. I was sure Lisa had said she kept it shut.

Our space was so tight at the top of the stairs, Persia's hot breath warmed my neck. This search would be quick. If a cat didn't answer our calls, we were out of there. I shifted my gaze slightly to see the outline of Persia's face in the gloom.

The door swung inward with a slight creak. We moved stiffly, holding hands in the dimness like a couple of children in a dreaded forest. A creepy chill lingered up here compared to the rest of the house, much like the mouldy air in an old fruit cellar. A small cottage window with four dirt-stained panes of glass offered the only source of light. The flashers from the emergency vehicles downstairs made it possible to pick out a few orange crates but, for the most part, the attic was empty.

"Here kitty, kitty," I cajoled, trying not to scare my quarry. My terse call echoed along the sloping ceiling. We had finally made it to the little window, when I heard a muffled mewling. I held my hand up to stop and we leaned in to listen.

"Look! There's something moving in the corner over there." Persia pointed. She moved a few steps ahead and bent to the dusty wooden planks. When she straightened up, her face jubilant, she cradled the littlest one.

"Nukkers." I breathed. "Jeez, Persia, can you see in the dark too?"

She giggled and offered me her free hand. Now that our eyes had adjusted to our dim surroundings, we made giant steps back to the stairs. I pulled the door as tight as it would go behind me. Relief flooded through me as we descended the stairs into the warmth and safe feeling of the landing. I made a cat count to calm my nerves, while Persia took her precious bundle toward the bedrooms.

"So, we have Montana in the master, Snappy and Hermie in the tiny bedroom and little Nukkers can keep Montana company," I called after her. "That leaves Sarge, Spruce, Haylow, Winky and"—I paused trying to remember—"Joey still at large. Let's go." I made for the staircase. Persia followed.

"Thanks for the help, cuz." I gasped at the bottom, rubbing my knee. "As it turned out, I was scared."

Donna held out bottles of cold water to us as we entered the kitchen.

"Reggie, I've looked all over the main floor and nothing. I heard you guys calling up there. Did you find any?"

"There's four upstairs. We put them in the master and smallest bedroom and shut the doors. Would you check on them at times? Lisa makes sure they have water and litter all ready for them in those rooms.

"Of course I will. Like you said earlier, there's lots of places here to lose things, and cats can sniff out great hiding spots." She looked us up and down, then made a nervous laugh.

"My God, you cat corralers are festooned in cobwebs. What a sight we all are." She gave a wide-mouthed yawn and pulled a hank of hair back from her face.

I gingerly touched my own hair, shuddering inwardly at the idea of spiders finding a new home. Looking around the downstairs rooms, it seemed hard to believe we had enjoyed ourselves there only a few hours before. My attention moved to the granite counters. With all the racket, the gray tabs who loved that space wouldn't be there. I felt sick at the thought. Then I caught myself.

"All we can do is our best. My fear is that they may have run past our cars into the forest. Lisa said something about predators attacking them if they did find their way out there. And now, I'm freaked. As if I'm not in enough trouble." I swiped the matted mess of hair back from my forehead and checked the perimeter of the kitchen.

"I saw a flashlight earlier somewhere, before the seance. Persia, can you find it and try another check outside? See if they're hiding under the deck or the cars. We just have to keep looking and hopefully gathering them up. Lisa will be a basket case if we don't find them all before they get home tomorrow."

Persia knotted her thick brows in concentration, then moved quickly to an antique chiffonier. She grabbed a yellow flashlight from a glass jelly jar and headed for the door as it swung inward. She stepped back as we beheld Dan bearing a squirmy, wild-eyed Haylow. She clung to his shoulder like a cat climber.

"Ouch!" he cried, his hand gently extricating her claws from his t-shirt. "Found this one under Persia's van, by the rear wheel."

"Haylow! Awesome, Dan, thanks!" I offered my hands to take her from him and gave him an update.

"We're over halfway there, thanks to you all. There are four cats safe upstairs and now number five. Donna's going to take care of them by keeping them safe in a couple of bedrooms away from the commotion."

A man's high tenor commands split through the yard noises. I went to the door to see who it was. Captain Cal held two big fingers up to one of the crew, who wrapped up the monstrous hose. Another firefighter retrieved the ladder that propped against the remaining garage wall. I walked over to him.

"More bad luck, Captain, there are four cats to find out here."

He looked sympathetic. "Hey, it's okay, Reggie, I just wanted to touch base with you before we left the premises." He lowered his voice and gave me a pat on the shoulder.

"Cats find their way home, especially cats in the country. How many?" he asked.

"There's nine altogether, and we managed to get five inside the house. They're indoor cats, not used to the country. They could easily get lost, especially with all this noise, the smoke, the fire! Oh, my God, I have to find them. My daughter will go crazy." Panic clawed up my throat.

He nodded at the garage where the flames were finally extinguished.

"We got this under control. Don't worry, even indoor cats have a way of showing up when you least expect it. We probably scared the bejesus out of them. You go ahead and look around and I'll tell the guys. Maybe they can help you search before we get out of here. Actually, I don't mind these structural fires." He turned for another look at the garage remains, then back to me.

I must have looked shocked by his words. He took off his plastic goggles and wiped the soot off them with a big thumb.

"No casualties," he said, sliding them back on.

"Hey, look who I found!"

I peered past the bulk of the captain to see Dan

coming out from under my front wheel well with another cat. I cheered at his good fortune and moved quickly to help him. Wide-eyed Sarge tried to wrestle his way out of Dan's arms, almost making an escape. I grabbed him by the scruff and hugged him close, then scurried to the door slipping quickly inside. I heaved a big sigh as he jumped to the floor and ran. That left Joey, Winky and Spruce.

While talking with Captain Cal, I'd lost track of Persia. I walked around the main floor, then recalled she had taken a flashlight to look under the deck out back. I returned to my search, crossing the driveway as a couple of firefighters gathering equipment, smiled and waved to me.

Then I saw her. She was deep in conversation with another firefighter by the old pergola at the edge of the garden. The lights from the trucks played over them through the wisteria leaves like actors in a stage play. He was the driver of the firetruck, the first to climb down. They went toward something in the dark. By the time I reached them, I made out a rusted, overturned wheelbarrow I hadn't noticed before.

"We heard yowling under here!" Persia cried out cheerfully, indicating the wheelbarrow. She turned to the firefighter who was watching her.

"Oh, by the way, Reggie, this is Gordon, the fire

truck driver. He said he can help us find the cats now the fire's been put out."

I shook Gordon's strong, hairy hand, then got down to the ground with caution to see which cat was hiding, my hands spread flat on the ground. Persia trained the flashlight on the interior to reveal none other than a spooked Spruce. I slowly reached my right hand out toward the frightened gray tabby, moved to my knee, and bit my lip as a hot bolt of pain shot through my leg.

I gasped, and took a deep breath, then got a hold on him and gave Spruce to Persia. Gordon offered his hand to help me to my feet. I wobbled like a drunk and silently cursed my bad knee. He gave me a look of empathy, his lips drawn in a tight line.

"I should have got that kitty," he said. "I know what that's like. My knees used to hurt like the devil. Then my daughter, a naturopath, turned me on to glucosamine supplements. Now my knees are a lot better, but I'm gonna get my first replacement after my retirement from the brigade next year. Won't be too soon either, ladies. This is a younger man's game. Damn college football." He chuckled, scratching his balding pate. Persia giggled.

"Thanks." I breathed and balanced against the wheelbarrow to brush dead leaves off my knees. I was starting to feel hopeful, even though my body felt like I'd been hit by a bus and my throat was on fire.

"Well guys," I spoke low for comfort. "We only have two left to find. Joey the gray and white hobbler and one-eyed Winky. Joey may not get too far. His front legs are shorter than his hind legs, so he can't move very fast." I paused to stroke Spruce's soft fur, then surprised myself as large tears coursed over my cheeks.

"I'm sorry." Embarrassed, I rubbed my eyes hastily. "But after all the sad backgrounds these poor creatures have survived... well, I just feel so badly about what's happened to them tonight. It's like that old Murphy's law thing. If anything bad can happen it will. Well, it has tonight in spades." I sniffed, wiping my nose on my cuff. It felt better just letting loose, even in front of a stranger. Persia regarded me.

"Lisa will never forgive me. Our relationship has never been ideal. I've always thought I didn't measure up fully as a mom. My job came first, it had to. I was a single mom with a jerk for an ex-husband. Now, years later, I wonder if there should have been more me and less daycare..."

Donna's ecstatic shout carried over the lawn. I could see her shadowed face lighting up in celebration, as we joined her raised hands for a high five.

"Good news everyone! I did another check in the house and found Joey hidden behind the clothes dryer. I had to use cat treats to get him to come out. What does that leave Reggie?" She shivered and pulled her sweater close, giving Spruce a scratch with one hand.

"Oh, thank God. Only Winky is left!" I whooped with joy in spite of my searing throat. It was possible. A daring thought that could save my bacon, crept into my mind. If I could find and bring Winklin home, maybe Lisa wouldn't have to know any cats got out at all. *Good thing cats can't speak.* But it meant finding that cat while I could still stand up. That time line was diminishing. Still, I put it on the back burner for future consideration.

Gordon and Persia snuggled Spruce. She pulled Gordon to her gaily, hugging him like an old friend. There was something weird about her. Weirder than usual. Maybe her bizarre new hairdo? I chalked it up to fatigue giddiness. God knows we were all entitled to that.

"See Reggie?" she sang, one sooty braid dangling like a dead mouse over her shoulder. With a deep dramatic breath, she presented her spiritual monologue, excited no doubt by Gordon's rapt attention. For once this evening, I was ready to listen.

"Just think, all the natural forces are uniting in this

celestial space, at this very moment in time. You hope, you pray, and you hand it over to God, your higher power, the universe, whatever you believe in. Remember when you were trying to get the garage door to open and couldn't do it? And you wondered where I disappeared to? Well, I searched all around and found a sacred spot by this very pergola. I sat on this very rock."

She placed her dirt-encrusted hand lovingly on a cement block and continued.

"I called upon my spirit guide to fill my soul with hope and fortitude. Once strengthened with the spirit guide's powers, I was able to go over to you all and raise the garage door. See, it wasn't all bad this evening. We are here for you Reggie. You have our love and support. Eight cats have now been found safe with only one kitty left. We will find him. I can feel it." She closed her eyes and glowed, enraptured by her thoughts. An odd smile played at the corners of Gordon's mouth.

"She's something, eh? I've never met a psychic before."

Persia emerged from what I assumed was a trance, gave an involuntary shudder, and rubbed her shoulders briskly. Once again, she was all business.

"So, which one is waiting to be found, Reggie?"

She gave me a sleepy grin.

"Winky… Winklin, the orange and white Persian." I looked over the yard.

There were three vehicles to our left: my Ford, Persia's van, and Lisa's car behind that. They had already been checked around and under. The house had been searched inside and out. There was no way the cats would have gone near the firetruck or garage. Cats weren't stupid.

I thought of all the activity and confusion that had taken place, not to mention the smoky haze which still hung heavily in the air. Maybe the smell of the smoke drove Winky away from the yard. What would he do with sudden freedom at night after three weeks indoors? Which direction would he go?

I had to think like a cat.

—oOo—

CHAPTER SEVENTEEN

Lisa's heavy limbs were dragged into a dim, damp place. She did not know where she was, only that her body felt compelled to go forward. Her numbed legs moved sluggishly like she was mired in a sea of molasses. Faint sounds ahead drew her forward, but she couldn't see where they were coming from. As she moved closer, they morphed into the muffled sounds of cat cries. Her breath became short rasps as her panic rose. Were they her cats? What was this place? Where was Brad?

She shouted into the darkness for help. The soft reverberation of her voice echoed down what seemed like a long, smelly chamber. Her fingers groped from side to side, blind until they finally made contact with slimy, wet stone.

The cats' crying amplified, growing insistent. Thoughts of how they might be lost like her or suffering in some unimaginable way assailed her. *Maybe they were being tortured.*

Angered by her impotence in getting to them, she forced herself forward, pulling one leg at a time through the swirling black muck. A loud sucking sound, an ear-splitting pop, and her body dropped without warning. Down, down she plummeted, wild arms and legs flailing through a black hollow. Within seconds, she landed hard on her back, knocking the wind out of her.

A hot glare of light exploded in her face. Trembling, she blinked to get some sense of her surroundings. Finally, she could see tell she was spread-eagled on the cedar deck of her new house. When Lisa raised her head, rock and roll boomed from an unseen source, while dozens of chattering guests mingled and swayed to a thudding drum beat. They were costumed in bold fluorescent colours, like a rainbow of dancing mannequins.

Lisa pushed herself up onto unsteady feet, then swooned. A heavyset woman dressed as a baby, complete with a frilly lace bonnet and plastic soother, took her by the arms and pinched them hard. Lisa cried out in pain, then shrank back from the woman-baby's leering, toothless face. No, it couldn't be. It was Marsha.

The music faded then stopped. Guests started a low hum which escalated into shrill peals of mirth. An irregular line formed, similar to the old bunny-hop dance, locking her into the centre. Wide clownish faces moved closer and closer until she had to strike her fists at them to escape. Sobbing, she forced her way past them to find herself in a lush field of waist-high grass.

Only, it wasn't really a field. It was the backyard of their new home. Brad hadn't cut the lawn and it was getting way too long. Then she saw them.

The tip of Winklin's long tail bobbed through the high grass. Snappy leaped after little Hermie who was playing hide and seek. Spruce came over to weave around Lisa's bare legs. She reached anxious hands to him, but he joyfully sprung away. They all ran through the fields of her backyard. Lisa saw the rest of them: Sarge, her big boy, followed by Joey, who struggled on his front legs, Montana, his big gray head following the others, then her girls, Haylow and little Nukkers, who was no longer little. They were all here in this place which was or wasn't her yard. She was having trouble understanding how they all got out of the house when she realized there was no cat fence. As if reading her mind, they ran farther away. She screamed for them to come back, but they gradually faded into a gray abyss, the black tip of Snappy's tail last to be seen.

The merry masqueraders on the deck guffawed louder and ogled her, their ugly mouths drawn up like scarlet flames. Lisa begged them to stop and help her find her cats. A hairy fingered, fat troll swaggered forward to pluck her from the field now engulfed in flames. A cloying burning smell assaulted her. It was her clothing. She screamed—

"Lisa! Lisa! Wake up!" Brad's voice broke through the nightmare.

She blinked her sleepy eyes at the strange room, then realized she was in their hotel room. He rocked her gently in his arms as she clung to him.

"Honey, what happened? That must have been some nightmare." He soothed her, then flicked on the bedside lamp to see her drenched face. His hand gently smoothed wet strands of hair from her forehead. She shook. He arranged the bed covers tighter around her.

"Oh, Brad, it was so awful." She choked out the words. "Our cats were running away through fields in our backyard. Oh God, there was no fence. Somehow, they all got out and were running away from me and all these horrible monsters were laughing. They were partying on our deck. Then the field was on fire. And Marsha was a baby!" She gave an involuntary shudder and snuggled into his shoulder. He regarded her in awe.

"Man, Lisa, that sounds crazy. No more green-apple cocktails for you," he teased and gave her a quick squeeze. "Shit, you scared the hell out of me. I thought you were being attacked in our bedroom. Then I saw we weren't at home. You better now, sweetie?" He kissed her cheek.

Lisa took a deep breath. "I think so. I guess I'm still worried about our kitties. I'll have a drink of water." She got up from the rumpled covers and went to the bathroom.

Brad stretched, groaning, then burrowed back to the warmth under the covers.

"Come on, honey. Crawl in here where it's warm. I promise I'll protect you from those boogey-people. Lisa?" He propped himself up on one arm. Lisa clutched her phone, eyeing the screen. She looked up quickly.

"Mom texted me. While we were at the bar. At midnight." She checked the message again then offered him the phone.

"But she didn't finish her message!"

He shifted his bulk off his elbow and twisted around to her for the phone.

"Lisa, I'm sorry," he read, then paused. Her wide eyes were dark hollows in the dim lamplight.

"Just a minute, Lise. Something's wrong here.

Maybe something with your phone? Your mother would call if there was an emergency. Maybe she just started to text to tell you something like, I'm sorry to message this late, but everything is fine."

She crashed headlong into the bed and collapsed, her face crumbling into tears. In one fast motion, she wrestled the phone from his fingers.

"I have to call her! Something's happened. She was cut off from messaging. She doesn't like texting, but she wouldn't leave me hanging like that. She knows I worry. Oh, Brad!" she wailed, hands trembling as she worked the keypad.

"Here, honey. I'll do it." He took the phone, hit the number, then held her hand as they waited.

"Lisa, it's some misunderstanding I'm sure. It's two in the morning. I really hate to wake your mom. If her cell is downstairs, she probably won't hear it anyway." He pulled her to him and they listened to the rings. When the voicemail cut in, he closed it and moved closer to stroke her hair. She jumped up from the bed and slapped him away.

"No, Brad! I know what you're going to say." She wrapped her arms around her waist like a straitjacket, then doubled over and began a low cry.

"Lisa, please, listen to me." He had only seconds to diffuse this.

"Your mom would have called us if there was an emergency. Even if her phone messed up, she could call us from Donna's phone. Just because she didn't finish a message doesn't mean there was anything bad happening. They're sound asleep upstairs in a big house. They wouldn't hear us call this late anyway. Jeez, your Mom's no night beast. She crashes by eight o'clock. And, let's face it, they've probably been quaffing all afternoon, having a grand old time. It's just a mix up. We'll get in touch first thing in the morning. Hey, we'll get up early, be on the road by eight."

Lisa stood stock still and stared at him. A flush of anger rose in her chest.

"No. We're going now. We can hurry home. There's hardly any traffic this time of night. I can't sleep anyway. You can sleep when we get back."

He rubbed a resigned hand over his mouth, stretched, and rolled his head on his shoulders. She was opposite him, arms crossed in defiance, auburn hair in disarray, daring him to cross the invisible line.

"We've been drinking," he said quietly, his last defence.

"I can drive!" Lisa tore open her overnight bag and tossed clothing into it.

"Stop! Just stop." He caught a sweater in mid-flight and flung it aside in frustration. "Come here." He crossed the room and took her hands in his.

She gazed up at him, her bottom lip trembling.

"I'm scared," she said in a small voice, then hung her head. He guided her over to their messy bed where they slumped looking at each other.

"I want you to take some slow deep breaths," he said, measuring his words.

She complied, starting slow regular breathing, a proven antidote in the past for her anxiety. He scooted back on the mattress, propping himself against the headboard, and pulled her gently to his chest. Her heart thrummed like a bird's through her pyjamas.

"Here, lay back with me. Get comfortable. Just breathe deeply and relax, babe."

"I'm sorry. You know how I get. I worry…"

"Shh, Shh," he murmured, rubbing her tight shoulder muscles. She uttered a tremulous breath, then curled her tense body to his, continuing the relaxation exercise. He spoke to her in a soft monotone. The little mantra always relaxed her in the past.

"Our cats are okay. Our cats are okay…" they repeated.

—o0o—

CHAPTER EIGHTEEN

Jessica left her Beemer in the farmers' market parking lot. She strode past the floodlit war memorial in the Dunnville town square. In contrast to the sedate, well-groomed homes down the street, the noisy sounds of Saturday night bands vibrated through shadowed bar doorways. There was an occasional catcall as she made her way past the local thirst-quenchers gathered out front to smoke their brains out.

Rick's buffed crimson Harley, the only thing he had to be proud of, sat parked at a sharp angle in front of the Blue Clover Inn. It was a dump like most of the other bars in town. The thought was tempting, but she couldn't bring herself to take a quick peek inside the place. Rick would be the first to loudly call out to her and everyone else if Dan had been there, then gleefully rub her nose in it. Rick was a liar and a fat loser anyway. Why Dan would bother with him was beyond her understanding, but he was his landlord and a friend before she was. She had a strong suspicion Dan wasn't there and hadn't been all evening. He would absorb his hurt in his own quiet way, and Rick would be no comfort to him. She returned to her car.

Dan's basement apartment was the next logical place to go, but she would just do a drive-by to see if any of his lights were on. His car, an old Dodge Dart, had been in the driveway for weeks, so there was no clue there. At Delhi Street, Jessica made a slow left and continued until she drew up opposite the one-story stucco monstrosity. A lone light in Rick's dismal rear kitchen cut through the blackness on the main floor. Dan's two cracked basement windows were dark and uninviting, but he could have crashed. He did seem tired that afternoon, or maybe wanted to avoid Rick's nosey questions.

She had to know if he was safe and at home. After parking her car quietly on the left side of the driveway, she picked her way to his bedroom window, dodging overfilled trash cans and dirty cardboard cartons spilling beer empties. His cheap plastic miniblinds were open, which wasn't a good sign. He wouldn't sleep unless they were closed. She attempted to peer through the window, one hand to the side of her face when the deafening roar of a motorcycle interrupted her surveillance and bright halogen light from its single beam exposed her.

"Woohoo! Looky what we got here!" Rick mocked as he struggled to pull his belly off the motorbike. "A regular peeping Tommy girl. Now, who would you be peepin' at, Jessie girl?" He belched loudly, then swaggered his bulk over to her.

Jessica froze then recoiled from his sour beer stench as he stuck his face into hers.

"You already know what I'm doing here. Don't be an ass. I need to find Dan." She lurched away from him, stumbling along the rutted driveway as fast as she could to her car.

"Well, he ain't lookin' for you darlin' that's for sure. He'd get an eyeful if he did. You look like shit," he called after her with a dirty laugh.

She jumped into the car, then gunned the engine to make a gravel-spitting pivot onto the silent street. When she looked back, he was still doubled over shaking with laughter.

Her breaths shortened as her anxiety ratcheted up. The sweet little pill case of Ativan beckoned from the Prada bag riding her hip. Jessica's frightened eyes shot to it then darted away.

No, tonight she needed a clear head. The dull brick facade of the police station loomed ahead on her right. She resisted the urge to park her car, drag herself in to the front desk, and give her sordid tale. It would be manned by a bored night cop, his pudgy hand propping up a tired face. He'd yawn, rub his baggy eyes, and send her on her way with the comforting words, *he'll show up. Probably on a Saturday night bender. We see it all the time.*

Her thin arms swerved the car recklessly onto a low grassy shoulder in a sleepy residential area. Jessica pressed her forehead onto the steering wheel in frustration. Where else would he go? Maybe he was just killing time with one of the guys in the band to avoid her. Who could blame him?

She sucked on a blue gel nail, then hit the steering wheel in anger, cracking her nail. Her blond head slumped to her chest like her neck had given up. A slow whimper rose from her throat, growing into a full-out sob.

It hit her hard, like a sucker punch.

There was no one to help her, no friend to call, and she didn't know what to do. Her eyes riveted to her throbbing finger. The broken nail looked hideous by the dashboard light. She considered pulling it off when a thought came out of nowhere.

What about driving back to the last place I saw him? The scene of the crime right, Jess? See if his body's in the ditch where you dumped him?

"Stop!" she cried, jerking the shifter into drive, pivoting the late model car back onto the road with a tire squeal.

A fortuitous street sign for Concession Eight loomed to her left, luminously directing her back to the winery. Even if it took the rest of this godforsaken night, she'd find him and beg for another chance. They could try couples counselling, or maybe a psychologist for her issues.

She didn't want to be her father's little girl anymore. It was time to make up her own mind about everything in her life, especially her relationship with Dan. The distant scream of an emergency vehicle startled her.

Instinctively, Jessica pulled off to the side of the road and waited. A fire truck roared past, its flashing red and yellow lights fading into the distance.

Jess recalled her earlier ride down this road with Dan in the bright, happy light of an autumn afternoon. It would be harder in the dark to see how far they had come earlier, so she had to look carefully.

The car's headlights flashed on a dead tree in the ditch, its white limbs pointing to the stars. Yes, she remembered seeing that. Another siren, shrill in the cool night air, filled her rear-view mirror with blinding lights. What was going on?

Within seconds another fire truck blew past her and made a right turn far ahead. She accelerated to catch up to them and see where they were going. As she slowed where they turned, her headlights picked up a long private driveway opposite a mailbox with cartoon cats painted on it. Jessica peered through the car window, catching flashes of emergency lights through the dense barrier of evergreens. The sirens had ceased wailing only to be replaced by the loud hum of motors and men's hurried exclamations. She maneuvered her car onto the embankment far past the driveway, where it wouldn't be so obvious, careful to skirt the steep ditch, then considered her next move.

She had the cover of night in this wooded area. Jessica glanced at her rumpled clothing – colourful but not a glaring white. The firefighters would be too busy being heroes to notice someone trespassing anyway.

Holding her breath, she shut her car door quietly. No other vehicles were visible in either direction of the road. Keeping her eyes to the ground, she plodded down the mossy ditch, cursing her Mahlon Blahniks, and wobbled like a drunk to the edge of a darkened driveway.

A sickening, burning stench made her sour stomach roil. The pink satin jacket did little to ward off the night's chill, but she pulled it tight across her chest, clutched her bag, and set out to slink along closely to the dim driveway on her right. In the shadowed shelter of the trees and bushes she figured there was no possibility of being seen should other emergency vehicles arrive. She jumped back as a fluffy, light coloured animal bolted past her. Probably some stray cat she figured as she got her breath back.

Too much time had passed since the afternoon's catastrophe. It didn't seem likely Dan would be on this property. To her knowledge, he didn't know anyone out this way, but Jessica had to find out for herself. Like the dumb saying went: leave no stone unturned. Maybe she could explain her situation to the rescuers after they did their job. Just like any other prying fire chaser, she wanted to see what was burning.

Moving with the stealth of a thief, her heels caught on the undergrowth. Jess attempted to lift her feet higher. The crack of a branch ahead echoed like a gunshot. The soft strap of her bag slipped from her shoulder. She swore and fell to her knees to find the purse. Thankfully, it had not rained for days and she felt only dry pine needles as she grabbed it and swung it back into place. Creeping silently from tree to tree, she could make out buildings lit up ahead.

A loud voice commanded orders, though it was hard to hear his words. Beyond the leafiness of her cover, a large brick manor loomed like a sleeping giant. An old hippie type van sat parked beside a dark SUV with a late model Lexus behind it. They were to the side of a ratty wooden porch that stretched the length of the three-storey house. On the other side of the house lay a long, black fire hose and various bundles of equipment.

Jessica pressed at her watering eyes with the heel of her hand and peered around a gnarled oak for a better view. The smoke lifted from the remains of a double car garage. Two yellow-jacketed firefighters steered an aerial ladder to the burning side of the building. With three walls gone, it didn't look like the garage would be saved.

Not that she cared. She'd never noticed the place before, stuck way out here, and she figured no one was hurt as there were no paramedic trucks around. Dan wasn't here anyway. Whoever was in the house, if anyone, wouldn't care about their fight that afternoon. They'd be more worried about the fire. A dumb idea to end a shitty night.

The burning smell stuck in her nose and no amount of rubbing helped. For the first time since she tramped through the woods, she took a moment to examine her appearance. What a joke. She looked like a skank. Her Versace cocktail dress was a wrinkled mess, stained at the hem with some god-awful slime, the exquisite tawny pantyhose a torn ruin and her hair felt like cotton candy. Totally yuck.

With one hand, she reached for a rough tree trunk to get her balance and pried off her favourite hot pink heels – turned – twin – torture – chambers. The relief overwhelmed her when swollen toes hit the cool cushion of pine needles. It would be all right just to hunker down and rest her body against the tree for a bit. She felt so tired. A quick check of her phone flashed a neon two a.m. at her. No one had contacted her. Not one person. She threw it into her purse, took a couple of deep breaths and closed her eyes.

"And that's the last time Carson went to that strip joint!"

Raucous male voices startled her, followed by a chorus of laughter. She blinked her eyes and roused herself. The air was cold, she couldn't feel her toes. It was time to get out of this place. Groping in the gloom around the tree, she located her shoes and shoulder bag. More male chatter drifted through the trees.

She froze, recognizing one laugh above the others. A deep, hardy laugh she hadn't heard in a long time.

—o0o—

CHAPTER NINETEEN

I had a hunch where the elusive Winklin might go and took off toward our cars. A female's cry split the air. My eyes darted to the dilapidated pergola, Persia could be extremely giddy in Gordon's company, or quite possibly hysterical for some other reason.

But that shrill cry didn't come from Persia. A wild-looking, skinny figure raced out from the trees. The woman threw herself full-force at Dan, a fancy designer bag connecting with the side of his head. He staggered, caught his balance, then grabbed her arms to save her from taking a face plant.

"What in the name of God! Who is that woman?" Captain Cal boomed to no one in particular, raising his hands upward.

Short of breath, I caught up to Donna who was as shocked as the captain.

"It looks like everything is coming to a head this evening," I observed.

From the pergola's direction, Persia strolled toward us, smiling to herself. She picked bits of debris from her dangling braid. Gordon followed close behind.

"I am a psychic, Captain, sir, but even if I was not gifted, I could tell you that that woman is Dan's girlfriend, Jessica."

Startled by her interruption, the captain looked away from the couple, to her, with a frown of consternation. She heaved a diva's sigh and made a dramatic gesture in the direction of the road with one sooty hand.

"They had a terrible argument this afternoon, you see, on the road out front, a little bit down from here. She was so upset that she dumped him out of her car and drove away. I came along shortly after on my way to share a vegan dinner with Reggie and Donna and saw this poor young man sitting in the dust at the side of the road.

"I stopped to see if he needed any help. He looked so dejected. As we talked and I got to know him better, an aura appeared just above his hairline. It had gray overtones which signified possible harm to his spirit, so I invited him here to join us for friendship and…" her voice trailed off when Captain Cal, seemingly not a fan of the spirit world, fixed her with a hard look then stuck out his bottom lip. He seemed about to comment, then trudged back to the trucks instead.

Persia followed his back, with pity. "There's something troubling him. I can sense it." She grasped her bloodstone pendant, which I was impressed to see had survived the rigors of our evening.

I caught Donna's look, and pressed my lips together to suppress a smile. I decided to go for it.

"Ok, cuz, I'll bite. What's bothering the captain, besides smoke inhalation, people spending the wee hours of the morning searching for cats, and a bit of unwanted gossip?"

"I suppose you're right. It's been an unusual evening, but this goes deeper, like a personal crisis of some origin. Maybe I should talk to him so I could open the—"

"Persia." Gordon had come up beside her with a friendly smile.

"I don't know how you do the things you do," he said carefully. "But Cal is just a very down-to-earth fella. He takes this volunteer work very seriously. I don't think he's ever met a pretty fortune teller before."

For the first time all evening, Persia looked at him speechless. I decided to take advantage of it.

"Okay guys. Thanks again, Gordon, for all your help. It was nice to meet you. Donna and I are heading inside to warm up. Persia, may I have the flashlight? I'm doing a final check for Winky before calling it a night."

Persia's gaze lingered on Gordon, then she turned to me and handed the flashlight over. Her far-away look made me think she was somewhere else. Given her personality, it could be a number of things: conjuring hope for Dan and Jessica, relief that this sorry night was almost over, or possibly the first stirrings of that crazy little thing called love.

"Persia really is something, isn't she?" Donna giggled, sneaking a look back at the pair as we walked to the porch.

"Yes, she is, but I wonder what at times. She's in her element tonight for sure. I'm waiting for her to pass out from fatigue or overstimulation."

Donna paused at the railing to pull out a stone from her shoe.

"I hate to even say it, Reggie, but could any more weirdness happen tonight?"

I groaned. "You're asking that of a woman who was raised by a Celtic mother and her superstitious sisters? After a night of incredibly bad luck? Do not tempt the gods of misfortune." I gave her arm a light squeeze, then pulled my hand away fast.

"Hey, you're like ice! Let's get inside and get some coffee going. I'll try one last Winky search, that's all I have left in me, much as I'd like to find him tonight. Isn't there a rhyme about the cat coming back the very next day?"

She tsked and rubbed her arms briskly as we hurried to the door. "This cat thing is getting to you, girl. You're quoting children's songs."

"You could be right. Maybe I just need a bit of warmth to bring me around." I held the outer door as she pushed the interior door open. The gust of warm air from inside felt wonderful. I resisted the temptation to go into the living room and curl up in my red chair.

"Want to have your coffee before you head back out?" Donna offered, already filling the glass decanter from the water cooler.

After attempting to tease out something yucky that had glommed onto my curls, I gave up and looked across the kitchen island.

"Better not." I shook my head. "I'll lose my ambition to get this done. If I sit, I won't get back up, but thanks. Just one last look. Shouldn't take long, then I'll be back for your brew." I turned to head back out.

"Think the love couple will be wanting some?"

"Looks like we may have two couples now. Our evening is turning into *The Love Boat*. Make lots!"

She laughed.

Once out in the cool air, I glanced in the young couple's direction. They sat closely on the bench, she held his hand and talked. They were oblivious to anything around them.

I had my own problems to sort out. It would take whatever energy I could summon to find that damn cat. People have never considered me to be a cat lover. I like pets in general, but this guy was my favourite from day one. Maybe it was that golden pirate eye, his noble Persian bearing, or simply his ongoing curiosity.

Lisa had voiced worry over the threat of wild animals in the forest and how light-coloured animals are easy prey. That stuck with me, and now I had this feeling that he may have headed there. Nothing psychic, just a strong, uneasy feeling.

Cats were nocturnal, they loved to hunt smaller animals, and there could be lots of hunting in that direction. There was an even chance that the high-spirited cat would head for the dark of the forest; after all, we had searched everywhere else and the lights and noise could have easily motivated him.

My hand tightened on the small yellow flashlight, one of those LED deals, which made it possible to illuminate far ahead. A definite advantage as this was a new area for me, probably for Lisa and Brad, too. The clean bouncing beam flooded the treeline where masses of burdock and thick dried weed made their claim. I lowered my head away from the pungent evergreens as I pushed through the bracken.

The hollow cry of a lone owl made me squint to see farther up ahead, but there was only dark stillness lit at intervals by the probe of my light. I thought of going back to the others for additional help, but they had done enough rescuing tonight. The final one would be mine, and I would do all in my power to make that happen. It was my headstrong Irish ancestry, I supposed. If I couldn't find him, I could tell my daughter I had done my best. Whether she ever talked to me again would be another matter. I decided not to dwell upon it and focused on my mission instead.

My ears attuned to every little crackle and crunch as my joggers took me deeper into the arboreous gloom. Sticky pine needles dug into my hair and clung like witch's claws. The tight balls of burdock were plentiful, releasing their brown spurs into my nylon jersey in clusters, pricking the skin beneath.

"Winklin. Winky," I called, the wheedling sound of my voice cutting the dead night air. I attempted to cry out louder, but it came out in a croak. My throat killed me; too much smoke and not enough water. The bright light cut a swath ahead, highlighting leering cracks in rotted old stumps along my forged path. How far should I go?

I came to a stop about fifty feet in. A small copse of tall oaks stood shining; their fire red leaves unusual through the host of pines. A soft rustling came from the dried grasses behind them. I sucked in a sharp breath as a lone cottontail, his eyes a pink flash, zigzagged away from my flashlight beam.

Standing very still, I listened past the cricket chirps for a cry through the trees. I thought I heard something: an intermittent sound, one that seemed close.

There it was again.

Heart hammering and face flushed with hope, I trained my light on the smaller oaks that bordered mature pines. Making my way over to the most imposing pine tree, I shone the light upward through its tangle of needles.

A small white and orange face, paled in the flashlight's beam, glared down at me. My adventurous friend had managed to make his way roughly ten feet up. I walked around the tree trunk, shining the light up to see if he was stuck. I would need to either coax him down or make my way up to him.

I tried my softest voice so he wouldn't climb higher, silently berating myself for not bringing the lure of cat kibble.

"Come on, Winky." I patted the branches closest to me. "Let's go home. I'll find some kitty treats for you."

The lone eye followed me warily; the pink mouth opened to meow.

I gauged the distance to him. I wasn't tall at five foot four inches, but seeing where he was situated, it didn't look impossible for me to climb. A couple of trial pulls on the branches at my level made me think they'd support my substantial weight for a firm toe hold. I wasn't in my best shape but would give it a go, maybe get the little devil to start moving his way down if he could. There was no way I could carry him; he'd make lunch meat out of me and I'd drop him.

From the direction of the house, an angry staccato of voices arose. I shifted my gaze off Winklin toward the conflict. Maybe Dan and Jessica had resumed their earlier fight. Then it occurred to me that in my haste to find the cat, I did not tell anyone exactly where I was going to look.

I stretched my foot up as high as I could, and got a good hold on the first branch about two feet up. It was painstakingly slow, cold fingers grasping each higher branch, the small flashlight clenched between my teeth like a lollipop. At the midway point, I willed myself not to look down but kept the small anxious face in my sights. He hadn't moved, the eye still fixed on my progress.

"Okay, I'm on my way up, you little baboon. I'll save you," I hissed around the flashlight.

The gap between us was only three feet now. Sweat broke out on my brow as I strained my arm forward to reach for him, panting with the effort. He shrank back, frightened by my advance with the bright light. My hand had just brushed his soft fur, so one more branch up would give me leverage to help him if he was wedged in, and hopefully get him to make his way down.

A grunt escaped me. My right foot flailed around for the next branch up. The sudden movement caused my other foot to slip off its branch. Panicked hands shot out for something to grab onto, but there was only air as I pin-wheeled down.

The flashlight spilled from my open mouth; lower

branches tore at me. I hit the ground with a jarring thud. A loud caterwaul hailed a hard thump on my chest before everything went black.

CHAPTER TWENTY

Dan couldn't believe it. One minute he was joking around with the guys as they piled equipment into the fire truck's storage lockers – for the first time since everything went nuts, he could feel himself unwinding – the next minute a woman screamed and Jessica came hurtling out of nowhere. Dan fell back in total shock.

He barely recognized her. The usual salon perfect hairdo was a dull, stringy mess. The hot gasp of her breath into his face was vile. Charcoal smears of mascara plastered around puffy, bloodshot eyes. The chic designer clothing she wore earlier looked tattered and dirty like she'd been in a catfight. Two firefighters behind them gaped in curiosity, then quickly averted their eyes to the jobs at hand.

"Hey, hey!" Dan disentangled her arms and held her away from him. She cried hard, her whole body shaking with the effort. He had to calm her down. How did she know where to find him?

"Come over here." He led the way to a paint-peeled bench that flanked what was left of the remaining garage wall, away from the firefighters.

Jittery, she squatted to sit, biting at her bottom lip.

"Shhh," he said, his hands ready to comfort her the way they always had. But the afternoon nastiness was still too fresh. He jammed his hands into his jean's pockets instead.

She straightened her shoulders and slid back on the bench. The familiar touch of her arm pressing his bicep did nothing to help his frustrations. He turned to her, hesitating with a sooty hand, then smoothed back her tangled hair. They were both in a state.

"How did you get here? I mean, how did you know I was here?"

Her eyes moved away from his to watch the red glow of the emergency lights. A soft hand crept into his. "I didn't know." She looked down at their entwined fingers. "All I wanted to do was find you so I could tell you how sorry I was. I'm such an idiot. But I was so angry at you. I thought you'd deceived me and that you'd made a fool out of me.

"I drove back to my apartment, took a sedative, and woke up after midnight. While I paced back and forth, I couldn't stop thinking about what had happened between us. I realized that I've been obsessed about finding you a job, trying to run your life, with my father's blessing of course. It's not fair to you. I've been looking for you all night to apologize. I even called Rick!" She hung her head.

"Bet that was an interesting conversation."

"I finally decided to return to the last place we were together. Like the scene of a crime, which in a way I suppose it was… My crime that is. Anyway, the fire trucks passed me, I could see them turn in here. So, I followed and parked farther down the road. I had nothing to lose.

"I didn't want to go home, so I crept through the woods along the driveway to see what the emergency was. I never thought I'd find you here. I still don't understand. Did you come here to use the phone? That was hours ago. Oh, God, I'm sorry. It was all my fault! I'm only relieved I found you tonight and that you're safe."

Dan rubbed his forehead to think about what she said, then craned his neck back to search the sky. A black outline of sharp evergreen peaks appeared in the east with the coming light of day. He made out the flanks of reeds that edged the pond, and the shining lines of the cars beside it. The air was chilly, but strangely he didn't feel cold. The smoke had gradually wisped away, leaving a dismal smell.

Men's voices hovered around the firetruck closest to them. It revved its engine a couple of times, signalling the rescuers' departure. Dan smiled in spite of himself at the one who joked giving him the thumbs up as they lumbered past. Across the yard, Persia wandered back to the house. Donna held the screen door open for her. He wondered if they'd found all the cats. Taking Jessica's hand again, he helped her up from the bench.

"We'll talk about this when we're feeling better. It's been a long night for everyone. I just want to go home. But first, I want to say goodbye to my new friends, some very amazing women."

His hand slipped away from hers as he walked over to the house, Jessica trailing a few steps behind. Waving an easy hand to the figures inside, he held the door open wide to let her enter first.

The big kitchen was very welcoming after the cold night air. Jessica made a quick appraisal of the two older women inside, one tall and blonde, the other skinny with messy braids. She figured they were about her father's age, maybe a rich gay couple who owned the place. Wordlessly, they stepped back to let the new arrival enter, their eyes curious. A strong smell of coffee and dinner lingered in the air. Jessica's stomach grumbled.

Dan gave a dry cough and cleared his throat as Donna closed the door behind them. A dull silence hovered as the women assessed each other. He finally broke it.

"Guess you figured out who this is, ladies." He nodded in Jessica's direction, then made the introductions.

"Jess, meet my friends, Donna and Persia."

Donna smiled at Jessica and ushered them to the stools at the kitchen island. "You must be so cold! How about some hot coffee? I just made it a little while ago."

"That would be awesome." He grinned at the offer while Jessica made a quick nod, swiveling her stool to get a better look at her surroundings. Persia watched her.

"I told Jess here that I really lucked out in meeting you all today." He pulled his stool closer to the counter and turned to Jess. "After what happened this afternoon, I was thinking of hitching back to town, but I'm glad I didn't. Persia came down the road at just the right time in her hippie van. She kindly invited me to share a vegan dinner with her cousin and her friend here. It's been great... well, except for the fire." He chuckled and picked up his coffee mug for a sip, then wiped his lips with the back of his hand.

Jessica sat silently trying to take it all in. She watched the women's attentiveness to Dan as he told their story.

"Persia is a psychic who reads palms," he gestured to his own hand. "Tarot cards, and other stuff. We had a seance after dinner. It was way cool. Donna is Reggie's closest friend since high school. Her late husband fronted a local band in the '60s so she is very into my kind of music. Reggie is one funny lady who does a great job entertaining guests. This place belongs to her daughter and son-in-law who are away overnight. They have nine cats. Just think, if you hadn't dumped me out of your car, I wouldn't have had this awesome day. Hey"—he leaned back on his stool to look up the staircase—"where is Reggie?"

"She's stubborn, right Persia?" Donna said, crossing resolute arms over her chest.

Persia nodded absently, entranced by the bloodstone pendant cradled in her hands. She rubbed it in a small circular motion with her thumb.

Donna groaned. "She went back out to find the last missing cat. The orange and white guy, Winky. That woman looked so worn out! I was hoping she would come in and try again later in the morning. But that's Reggie." She turned away to check the microwave clock behind her. "It was half an hour ago. She said she wouldn't be long." Donna paced the kitchen, rubbing her hands together.

Persia slipped quietly from her stool, a worried look in her eyes. "I gave her my flashlight when I was outside. She didn't tell me where she was going. We need to search for her. Now."

The low drone of a motor broke the quiet outside. Donna dashed to the front window. A maroon SUV pulled in, its halogen lights flashing on the line of kitchen-cupboard doors as it pulled up to the remains of the garage in a crunch of stone. The engine died.

Donna turned to face them, eyes wide.

"My God," she whispered. "It's Lisa and Brad!"

—oOo—

CHAPTER TWENTY-ONE

The horrified couple flanked either side of their SUV staring at the blackened ruins of their garage. A low guttural moan escaped Lisa. Her eyes squeezed shut, wild arms reaching for her husband's. Brad rushed over, splashing through muddy water and held her.

"I won't look at this, Brad! This hasn't happened!" She reached for his jacket collar, wiped her runny nose, then craned her neck to eye the ruin.

"I knew it! I knew it! You wouldn't listen to me until it was too late and now our garage is burnt to the ground!"

Her knees buckled. She collapsed to the ground sobbing, her short legs splayed out like a marionette with its strings suddenly severed.

The screen door smacked shut, expelling the four bewildered guests. Donna ran toward them, wringing her hands.

"My God, Lisa. Brad. Please listen to me. This

was not Reggie's fault... or mine." Donna watched Lisa, who sat squinting up at her from the ground.

"Where's my mother?" she demanded, her lips forming a tight line. Lisa twisted her head around to glare at the watchers on the porch.

"Persia?" she cried out. "What is going on? Who are these people? This is crazy!" She looked back at Donna. "I want my mother to explain this, not you. Where is she?" Lisa howled, then challenged the spectators. "Are you hiding her? She should be hiding. What are you doing in our house? Who are you people?"

Brad moved swiftly to take her arms and force her to stand, but she shied away from him digging her black flats into the stones. He winced, letting her down carefully.

"Honey, come on. You are having an episode on our dirty, wet driveway. Uh, Lisa?"

She pushed him away with one vicious hand and remained rooted to the spot.

Sighing in defeat, Donna straightened, then fixed Brad with a worried look. "This can all be explained. The main thing right now is to find Reggie. She left the house in search of the last cat, but..."

Too late, she realized her mistake. Her hand flew to her mouth as she waited for the coming reaction.

Lisa's head popped up and as if magically energized, she jumped to her feet. "What last cat?" She grabbed Donna's arm with hard muddy fingers. Her brown eyes bugged out in shock.

"What are you talking about? The cats got out?" She screamed, then fled to the front door. Donna broke away to follow, but Brad's hand held her back.

"Let her go. She needs to see for herself that the cats are okay. We had a terrible night in Toronto. She was hell-bent on getting home. Then this. Did the firefighters say anything about how it started? Wait, never mind, let's find Reggie and..." he paused. "Which cat?"

Dan came forward, wiped a dirty hand on his jeans and offered it to Brad.

"I'm Dan Riverton. I feel bad you had to come home to this. It wasn't anyone here's fault. I heard the firefighters say it might be dry brush and all that."

Persia nodded and walked up to Brad. "I can explain why we're all here." She held her pendant tightly to her chest. "You see, Reggie was supposed to have lunch with me today, but she got the dates mixed up, so she invited me here instead. Dan is a friend of ours, and that girl there is his, umm, friend Jessica. He helped us save Lisa's car... and find the cats that got out when we tried to put out the fire... after Reggie called 911," she finished.

Brad spied the Lexus by the side of the house.

"Christ, her car! How did you ever...?" he was interrupted by the loud return of Lisa.

"Our poor kitties are so scared upstairs!" Her voice came out in a high-pitched whine. "They may never get over this. I looked all over the house and couldn't find Winklin. My baby. We have to find him!" Lisa absently curled her hair around her finger.

Donna stormed up to her, uttering an incredulous gasp.

"What about your mother? My God. We have to find her! She went back out to look for that damn cat. After this unbelievable night, I'm amazed she had the will or energy to do it. Between trying to put out the fire, pushing your car out of the burning garage, and searching all over the property and the house for your cats, she didn't stop."

Lisa's dark eyes hardened as she lashed back.

"Well maybe if she hadn't invited a bunch of people over to party here, none of this would have happened!"

Donna fisted her hands at her thighs, her flushed face close to Lisa's.

"You have got to be kidding," she spat. "I can't believe how selfish you—"

A yowl and a flash of fur flew past as Winklin headed for the front door. Lisa joyfully raced after him. He mewled, moving back and forth under the bright porch lights. The others watched her in awe.

"My baby boy! Honey, are you okay?" she crooned, her two quick arms scooping him up from the doorway. Relieved, she buried her face in his fur. He rewarded her with a well-placed swipe of his front paw to her cheek.

"No, honey. That's not nice. I know you're upset..." her high, singsong voice faded as she disappeared through the doorway, the cat clinging like a burr to her shoulder.

Donna watched for a few seconds, then walked over to Brad. She brushed her hair back with a weary hand.

"Look, I'm sorry. I realize that Lisa's upset about the cats and everything that has happened tonight but—"

"Say no more. Lisa can be very difficult at times. Her ability to manage her stress has been sorely tested this evening."

He turned to the bedraggled group watching. "Look, there's no problem with Reggie having family or friends over to our place whether we are here or not. It's not like she's a reckless teenager inviting strangers into our home. The garage was insured. It'll be replaced, but Reggie can't be, so let's get moving.

"We'll check the forest over there, first. It goes the deepest to our property, maybe a hundred metres. Obviously, she's out of hearing distance or is unable to respond. Let's not panic. It'll be hard enough for me to handle Lisa. Give me a minute to grab a high-beam searchlight from the car."

They stood mute as he returned with the flashlight and a plaid car blanket. Lisa, breathless, ran up to join him. She wore a satisfied look on her face. Her shoes scuffed loudly on the stones.

"I've checked the kitties. I got them all safe downstairs now. At first, they just hid from me until I started talking to them so they would know their mommy was back home. Then they all ran downstairs."

She paused, then arched her neck to look over the group to the dim treeline.

"Isn't Mom back yet? I thought she chased Winklin out of the trees. Where is she?" She eyed Donna and the others warily.

"We're going to find her right now." Brad explained in a calm voice. "You can help by staying close to me and calling out for your mom. I have a strong, high-beam here"—he held up his heavy-duty searchlight—"that she'll see so she'll know we're coming for her."

"No!" she snapped and bolted like a jackrabbit toward the forest. "I'll find her. Mom! Mom! Winklin came home! He's okay. Where are you, Mom?" Her words faded in the early morning air as she vanished into the bushes.

Exasperated, Brad hollered. "Wait for me! It's dark in there and you won't be able to find her without a light!"

He dropped the flashlight and held his head in both hands.

"Goddammit! I hope we find Reggie soon. Though I don't think Lisa will go far." He swore again, then resumed his plan with a sigh. "Okay everyone, let's start a line search. Stay across from each other and fan out a bit. Keep calling out, eyes to the ground."

He trained the luminous beam ahead, making a wide sweep of the area. It picked up Lisa's blue jacket moving through the trees.

"Stay right there, Lisa, we're coming."

Donna and Persia grimly pressed forward, holding back small branches for each other. They stayed within sight of the beam as it bounced eerily ahead, giving a ghostly appearance through the vegetation.

Dan's rasped entreaties for Reggie. Jessica's echoes joined him.

Thirty feet in, Brad discovered his wife hovering by the base of an uprooted tree. Her trembling, white hands covered her face. She shook silently. Moving past the broken branches, Brad came up to hold her.

"It's all my fault, isn't it?" She spoke in a dull defeated whisper.

"It's no one's fault, Lisa." He whispered into her soft hair. "We'll find your mom, I promise. Just stay with me, okay? We have lots of help and we'll just keep moving ahead."

Further up, Donna and Persia spoke in hushed tones as they made slow progress through the skinny saplings with whip like branches.

"Reggie!" Donna cried again. The smoke of the evening was finally taking its toll on her voice. Persia reached out through the dimness and gingerly touched her.

"I won't say anything to the others, but I know she will be found… hurt, but alive."

"Oh, my God. I hope you're right." Donna reached for Persia's frigid hand while fighting back tears.

"I should have insisted she stay at the house. Reggie! Where are you?"

Persia moved alongside Donna, sweeping back stalks of weeds with a careful hand.

On the far side of the women, Dan helped Jessica over some deadfall. She slipped on the damp moss and fell to one knee.

"Crap!" she cried, pushing herself up from the black muck.

"Jesus, you okay? It's hard to see where we're going." He helped her stand unsteadily, then took her hand as they located the beam up ahead.

"This is unreal," he muttered. "I have to tell you, I'm freaked out. She seems tough, but she is older and, well, she's been through so much tonight. I keep thinking she may have had a heart attack or a stroke."

There was a shout. Hands clasped tighter, the couple stumbled along in the direction of more cries and the brightness of the light which they could see Brad holding now.

"I see something over there! A light on the ground!" Persia called as they caught up to her and Donna.

Brad's flashlight beam moved to a cluster of oaks and pine. A small flashlight lay upended at the base of one of the fir trees. Its upward glow illuminated high branches dense with dark needles. Dan bent over to pick it up when his eyes caught something yellow a few feet from the tree.

Reggie.

As he crept closer to the still form, he could see that she was sprawled on her back, eyes closed, her face lacerated with small cuts. Her right arm was wedged under her back, one leg bent at an awkward angle over the other.

Lisa rushed to her mother, screaming, while the others stood immobilized.

"She's dead! I killed her! I shouldn't have asked her to look after my cats! Mommeeee!" She flailed her arms and fell onto her hands and knees.

In two quick strides, Persia reached Lisa and took her in her arms. Lisa buried her face in her cousin's shoulder and sobbed convulsively. Donna kneeled next to her friend, stroking her curls.

"Reggie? Reggie?" Brad whispered, pressing two fingers to the pulse point of his mother-in-law's neck. Her body was still warm, a good sign. Adjusting the car blanket gently around her, he breathed a sigh and punched 911 on his phone. He called over to Lisa.

"Listen to me, Lisa. Your Mom is alive. She's unconscious, but the ambulance is on its way. Do you hear me? She's breathing. Just stay there with Persia."

Brad kept one cautious eye on her as he finished

the dispatch information. Dan left Jessica by the women to approach him.

"Hey, want me to stand out front of the house?" He gave Reggie a worried look. "When the ambulance gets here, I can show them exactly where you are."

Brad gave a grateful thumbs up as Dan ran back through the trees.

Donna rubbed Reggie's hand softly.

Brad spoke in a low voice. "Are you good with going to the hospital? I can't leave Lisa here alone, and she sure wouldn't be any help there. I can come and join you once I get her to sleep."

Donna sniffed and nodded. "You know I will. I want to be there when she regains consciousness."

"Mom... Mommy..." Lisa repeated the words over and over while she looked away from her mother's still form. His instinct was to go to her, but he stayed by Reggie's side. Lisa still clung to Persia, as Jessica watched nearby, entranced.

"Ladies!" he ordered. "I need some quick help here. Lisa is hysterical. Persia, do me a big favour and get her back to the house any way you can. Tell her she needs to check on the cats, whatever. We'll stay here until the ambulance comes. And Persia?"

She pivoted back from her hold on Lisa to look at him.

He rubbed a hand over his face. "Would you please give her a stiff drink?"

She nodded, then led Lisa away.

"Wait for me!" Jessica called after them, rummaging through her shoulder bag. "I can do better than a drink."

—o0o—

EPILOGUE

"**O**h, she's beautiful!" Persia exclaimed, cupping Donna's phone in her careful hands.

I watched, amused by the two of them, as I lay back on a comfy rattan lounger.

"And this one!" Donna crowed, pointing to yet another photo from our trip to Vancouver. Persia looked over at me with a giggle.

"Hide and seek with Auntie Reggie." She beamed. "Just like when Lisa was a little tyke. Toddlers are so much fun! Even grumpy people get silly with them."

"I was only grumpy with the security authorities," I protested, reaching for a handful of lentil chips. "It's so invasive getting your goods searched," I grumbled. "The arrogance of the authorities is appalling compared to the last time I got on a plane."

I stuck out my lips and crunched noisily. Donna laughed at my drama and threw a chip at me. Persia tilted her silver head to one side and squinted through her wire rims to consider.

"Yes, I believe that was in the eighties, right?"

I stuck out my tongue at her. "Okay, it's been a while," I sniffed. "But that may change. I now have the incentive to vacation and explore the world. With my traveller-friend of course." I motioned to Donna. She glanced up from her phone.

"All she needs is first class and lots of liquid sustenance. The more she flies, the more comfortable she'll become with it. Though I must admit, my future travels will mostly be to the West Coast."

"Say the word and I'm in," I offered. "Four adults and one adorable little doll to spoil works for me." I stretched out my stiff legs, then teased. "Get comfy, cuz, Nana Cairns has three hundred more to show you."

Donna and I had recently returned from a ten-day visit to Kevin and Leo's incredible oceanfront condo. A month ago, Donna was thrilled to learn that she was a new grandmother to little Taya. The guys had waited to tell her the good news until the adoption proceedings were finalized and they returned from Beijing. Donna asked me to be with her when she held her little granddaughter for the first time.

It was a momentous occasion. We arrived at Vancouver International Airport, entered the waiting area, and there they were. Kevin and Leo, ebullient as they held the little red-jacketed girl up to us. Donna rushed forward, arms outstretched, laughing and crying at the same time. I fumbled with my phone, trying to get a good group shot in spite of my own tears. I'd never seen Leo so animated. He gave me a happy wink, then proceeded to cuddle in with the others for the photo.

I drifted into lazy contentment as they chatted happily, Donna's low drone contrasting with Persia's soft soprano. Our October afternoon was bathed in buttery sunlight. It dappled the bleached husks of summer garden vegetation along the low picket fence. The old stone birdbath we gave Persia for a housewarming gift had a special place of honour under two towering red maples. As my eyes wandered over the leaf-strewn yard, I could see why the quaint cottage, with its large, sunny porch attracted her bohemian eye. The perfect backdrop for her hocus pocus, as Dan would say.

As promised, our young musician friend had kept in touch. In his latest email, he discussed promoting his new demo recording through a friend in Toronto he was temporarily living with. Dan was now a solo act on the coffeehouse circuit, where he blended arrangements of folk and jazz. He made money on the side too, teaching guitar to all ages. Although Donna and I were dying to ask about Jessica, we agreed not to. It turned out to be a good decision as we found out much later, online, that Jessica had eloped with an onion farmer from Woodstock. Apparently, they had joined forces to discover a secret ingredient in that smelly vegetable to promote younger-looking skin. I had yet to try it.

Lisa and Brad were adjusting well to country living. Thanks to a generous insurance settlement, their brand-new reclaimed brick garage was an architect's dream – a modern take on colonial style with narrow crescent windows, two metal automatic doors, and a huge second floor they are thinking about using as a workout room. Brad ribbed me, suggesting that I could create my own library by living there and adding to my extensive book collection. I think he knows that I might've taken him up on the offer at one time, to be closer to my daughter, but things are different now.

Lisa was finally able to emerge from her cocoon of obsession and anxiety to become a relaxed, independent woman. The transformation was slow and not without difficulty – for her as well as Brad. In one quiet moment when we were alone, he confided that it almost cost them their marriage.

Through classes in meditation and yoga, Lisa

gradually learned breathing exercises for calming, as well as the value of positive thinking. So much so, that she entered a six-month program and became a certified yoga/meditation instructor. She worked part-time at a salt-cave spa, which enabled her to make new friendships locally.

One of her best discoveries was that her cats would survive her absences; that the break from them was actually good for all. She still had her hand in rescue work, through freelance magazine articles. Through the Pause for Claws grapevine, she learned that Muriel's drink had been tampered with and there was an ongoing police investigation. After this news and Muriel's subsequent resignation, Lisa and Brad decided to retire from the organization. Lisa maintained a correspondence with her grandmotherly friend and, last I heard, Muriel planned to visit them over the Christmas holidays.

A year ago, Persia advised me that all would be revealed in time. I don't consider myself to be religious or spiritual, but I think she may have had something there. The fall from the tree gave me more than a mild concussion, a fractured arm and three cracked ribs. My gradual recovery allowed me to watch Lisa mature and grow in confidence.

She visited regularly to check my progress and do

the lifting and household tasks I couldn't manage. For the first time, I realized I didn't have to worry about her as I had before. It was liberating for both of us.

"Reggie. Earth to Reggie!" Startled from my laidback reverie, I laughed at the two of them waving their frantic hands in my direction.

"Where were you?" Donna asked, smiling. "You looked light-years away."

I shifted my position on the lounger. My left foot had fallen asleep.

"Just daydreaming." I puffed out a sigh and leaned over to rub my numb foot. I shot a quick look at Persia. "Say, gypsy woman, weren't we invited here for drinks as well as dinner?" I made a big show of looking around the wide veranda.

On cue, the screen door fell open and out stepped Gordon, bearing a bamboo tray of tall wine glasses, topped with tiny cocktail umbrellas.

"A cabana boy special, ladies." He bowed ceremoniously before us; his bushy gray moustache curled up in a grin. Over the months, he had allowed his receding hair to grow longer. It was pulled back into a gleaming ponytail. He looked exuberant.

"This is my lovely Persia's recipe for organic ruby Sangria, and my first time mixing it. I hope it makes your taste buds dance!" He gestured grandly with a large hand to the tray. We giggled at his theatrics like teenage girls, oohing and aahing at his presentation. He gave a quick salute, blew a kiss to my cousin, and went back inside.

"Just checking the chili and the leaderboard," he called back to us.

Donna turned to Persia awestruck.

"Did he just say *Ouija* board?" she said, her eyes wide.

I laughed so hard I broke into a coughing fit.

"No, Donna," Persia answered sagely. "Let's get this straight, my dear. He said leaderboard, as in golf. He's the golf nut, while I'm the psychic nut."

We all laughed. She moved forward to take one of the wine glasses, appraising it with an arched eyebrow.

"Now, let's see how good his mixing skills are." We followed suit, taking the whimsical drinks in hand.

I raised my hand to interrupt.

"First, a toast." I gave Donna a wink.

In the fading afternoon light, I proclaimed, "To journeys. Past, present and future."

—o0o—

KITTY BIOS

HAYLOW

Haylow is a warm hearted tabby who was rescued at a young age in a church. She was adopted in 2013.

SARGE

Sarge, the biggest of the cats at 18 pounds, was rescued in a litter of five. He was adopted in 2013.

NUKKERS

Nukkers (Jannuka) This "little girl"
was found with two sister kittens.
She was very skittish, but has adjusted well. She was adopted in 2013.

MONTANA

Montana, another big guy, was rescued from a hunter's trap causing him to lose his left front leg. He was adopted in 2013.

SPRUCE

Spruce, rescued as a young cat, is always on the prowl for small critters. He was adopted in 2013.

SNAPPY

Snappy, the black and white jumper,
was rescued twice. He is very friendly
and was adopted in 2014.

WINKLIN

Winklin, the distinctive orange and white part Persian was rescued at a college campus. He lost his left eye due to a severe upper respiratory infection as a kitten. He was adopted in 2016.

JOEY

Joey is a Squitten. He was born with a genetic deformity, making his front legs shorter than his hind legs. This is often due to inbreeding. He was adopted in 2016.

HERMIE

Hermie (Herman) was a kitten rescued from a hoarding situation of over 100 felines. This timid boy was adopted in 2018.

Thank you for coming on this journey with me.

Keep in touch! Please feel free to leave a review on JudithRead.com, facebook.com/JudithReadAuthor, or on Goodreads.

ABOUT THE AUTHOR

Judith Read is a native of Welland, Ontario. She is the author of "The Boomer Years: Reflections." Her love of nostalgia and writing has earned her recognition; a short story inclusion in the 2008, "Frontiers" anthology in British Columbia and a first prize in poetry in an all Ontario competition in 2020. She has three daughters, a grandson and a granddaughter. This is her first novel.

Made in the USA
Monee, IL
29 December 2020